Currents Of Change

Darian Smith

ISBN: 978-0-473-31810-9

This book is a work of fiction and any similarity to anyone, alive or dead, is purely coincidental.

ACKNOWLEDGEMENTS

I'd like to say thank you to my wife, Adrienne, for her support, advice, and willingness to feed me chocolate during the writing of this book.

I'd also like to thank Carolyn Smith-Masefield and Victoria Dreyer for their help with editing, formatting, and such sundries. I am incredibly fortunate to be surrounded by a community of supportive writers.

CHAPTER ONE

Sara's fingers gripped the wheel, convulsing on it like a live electrical wire. The speedometer crept higher. Five…ten…twenty kilometres over the speed limit.

Gorse, clay, and punga trees merged into a green and yellow blur at the edge of a road that was cut into the face of the hillside like a tar sealed scab on Mother Earth. A scar that would never heal on Papatuanuku's wild green skin.

She kept her eyes fixed on the road and her jaw clenched until the distracting buzz of her phone fell quiet and she could breathe again.

So much for silent mode. She should have switched the damn thing off.

She swallowed, relaxed her fingers, and eased her foot back off the pedal, just a bit. Just a tiny bit.

The car crested the top of the hill and began the descent into the valley below. For a moment she got a glimpse of farmland stretched out like a blanket and the blue sparkle of the sea beyond that. Then the trees rose up again and shadow covered the road.

She'd been driving for hours. Since well before

dawn when even the city had an eerie, deserted feeling about it. It was a feeling that extended well into the bush and tiny country towns that were all she'd seen since lunch. She hoped it would be deserted enough.

The world had potential in it – like the ocean she had glimpsed in the distance. There was sunlight somewhere, and she could get to it now. She had to believe that. To cling to it. She would find what she needed soon. The sacrifice had been too great otherwise.

She flicked the switch on the door and the driver's side window slowly wound itself down to let in the wind. The cool air buffeted her hair and face, cleansing and free, until she was trembling with cold, but her skin tingled with exhilaration. She had done what she needed to do. She was free.

A light flashed on the side of the road, bright and startling.

"Shit!"

She hit the brakes but it was too late. She hadn't realised how quickly her speed had crept up again. She glanced in the rear-view mirror. Sure enough, a speed camera vehicle sat tucked into the trees like a spider waiting for her unwary flight.

"Damn it." What speed had she been going?

She flicked the switch again and the window wound its way up. Her skin warmed quickly. She should have known better. Her mind began working on ways she could hide what she had done – ways she could pay the fine and keep safe.

Then it struck her: she didn't have to. It wasn't her vehicle anyway and she was already safe.

Already safe! The words echoed in her mind like

something forbidden. Like blaspheming the laws of nature. The absurdity of it fizzed in her like a chemical reaction and she found herself laughing. Laughing in great gulping breaths that tore at her insides, where she wasn't quite healed, and cramped her stomach with pain but somehow she couldn't stop. She pulled the car over to the side of the road and yanked on the handbrake while the shuddering mirth ripped through her body. Sobs mixed into the laughter and suddenly she found she was crying. Crying and shuddering like a madwoman. Insane.

She clutched at her hurting stomach and tried to slow the sobs. She pushed the emotions down, forcing air into her lungs, deep and even. In through the nose, out through the mouth. That's what the counsellor had told her. For once Sara was glad she'd been visited by the woman. No matter what she might have told the nurses and doctors when she'd left, at least this simple mantra seemed to help.

In through the nose, out through the mouth.

Breathe in. Breathe out.

She swallowed the last of the emotion down and closed her eyes for just a moment.

It wasn't far to go now. She was nearly there.

"Come on, Sara," she told herself, her voice little more than a whisper. "Sort your shit out."

Her stomach ached still and she wondered if she was bleeding. No point stopping to check now. She'd deal with it when she got to her destination. She put the car into gear and accelerated out onto the road.

An hour later, the town of Kowhiowhio was a blip on the highway, just north of the Bay of Islands. She hadn't found it on a map. Even her GPS had struggled, only giving her a nearby intersection of the highway. If she hadn't been given a description of what to look out for she'd have driven right past it.

Wide green paddocks gave way to a sudden burst of shops and houses, like paint drops spattered on green carpet. There was a petrol station, a pub, a convenience store with its familiar aproned grocer beckoning from the sign on the eaves, and a few others.

"Kowhiowhio Four Square," read the sign. This was the place.

Sara pulled over and parked the car. Her grandmother's words echoed in her head. "Once you get there, ask the locals. They'll know where it is. It's a bit of a town landmark."

She pushed the car door open and dragged her aching body out onto the footpath. A town this size couldn't have too many landmarks but even here it seemed strange for an empty old house to make the list. She put her hands on her hips and arched her back in a stretch. Her stomach still hurt but not as badly as she'd feared.

Straightening up, she tucked a strand of dark hair behind her ear, then reconsidered and pulled it forward again to hide her cheekbones. She glanced at her phone. The screen glowed with notifications of missed calls and text messages. She slipped it into her handbag and strode into the store.

The layout was similar to most country dairies, if a little larger than most. It likely served as the local supermarket – if such a word could be applied to a shop this size. To the left, an internal door connected to the fish and chip shop next door. On the right, a segregated booth held a sign proclaiming, "Nate's Electrical" and had spools of cable on a counter but no attendant. In the main section of the store, shelves ran in straight lines with a clear path to the checkout counter.

Sara paused to pick out a few items of food. She was going to have to eat while she was here, after all. Something quick and easy for tonight, and something for tomorrow's breakfast. She'd come back and do a proper, healthier shop in the morning. She couldn't face much more than that right now and anyway the doctor had told her to rest up. She tried not to imagine what he'd say if he knew she'd been driving all day.

She grabbed a couple of tins of spaghetti, some cereal and milk. Then, as an afterthought, picked up a vegetable and fruit juice concoction in a small glass bottle as her nod toward at least attempted nutrition. Her arms full, she made her way up to the counter.

A handsome man in his mid-thirties was talking to the shop clerk. He was tall and rugged with dark hair that was just a little too long and stubble across his strong jaw. He wore jeans, a polo shirt with "Nate's Electrical" embroidered on it, and a troubled expression.

"You don't think she's up for it?" he said.

The woman behind the counter shook her head, her black hair pulled back from her face in a ponytail that bobbed with the movement. She was a Maori woman in her early forties with a tribal band tattooed around her wrist. "She needs to learn responsibility first or you'll have trouble on your hands. I think you need to learn more about how little girls think. You're floundering. You have been ever since Em died."

"Actually, Moana, I think I've done pretty well."

"You would."

His jaw tightened, strength evident in the line of the muscles there. "Meaning?"

The woman opened her mouth to answer, then caught sight of Sara. She frowned. "Yes?"

Sara felt her face get hot. She lifted the groceries in her arms. "Sorry to interrupt."

The man turned away.

"No problem," the woman said, still eyeing Sara suspiciously, as though she'd intentionally been eavesdropping. "Haven't seen you before. You passing through?"

Sara dropped the items on the counter and watched as Moana scanned each one. "Actually, I'm going to be staying in town for a while. At the old O'Neill house. Do you know it?"

Moana set a tin of spaghetti down with a bang. "Are you serious?"

Sara licked her lips, her mouth suddenly dry. "Yeah. Why?"

The scanner beeped twice before the woman spoke again. "No one with half a brain goes there, girl. That's a bad place."

Sara felt her fingers curl into fists. "And why is that?"

"Just don't stay there. It's a run-down dump of a place anyway. Why would you want to live there?"

A range of answers ran through Sara's head.

Because it's my family home.

Because I have nowhere else to go.

Because this whole town is a run-down dump so

what's the difference? At least no one will find me and I'll be safe.

She was tired – so tired – and sore inside and out. This day – this whole nightmare – had gone on long enough. Frustration turned into belligerence and before she could moderate it, the words spilled out of her mouth. "Well that's my business, isn't it?" She threw the money on the counter and picked up her bag of groceries. "Can you give me directions or not?"

Moana's jaw dropped.

It was the man who answered, an amused twinkle in his bright blue eyes. "Head north from here, take the first road on your left, then the third right. It's a gravel road, looks like a driveway. The O'Neill place is right at the end."

Sara forced herself to nod graciously. "Thank you." She turned on her heel and walked back to the car.

"Don't blame me if the ghosts come for you in the night," Moana's voice called out as she reached the door.

Sara felt the echo of her earlier hysteria bubbling in her chest. Ghosts were the least of her worries.

CHAPTER TWO

The house was practically a ruin. The paint was peeling and a few of the windows were cracked. The grass was as high as Sara's waist and barely parted to make way for the gravel driveway. Closer to the house, where there was once a garden, gorse and privet had conquered roses, their spiked skeletons brown and dead. Wisteria crept up the right hand side of the house, up two stories and onto the roof.

The property backed onto rugged, native bush on one side, and an overgrown orchard on the other. The unsealed road had just two other homes on it, spread wide apart and in considerably better condition than this one. Bumping over the potholes, she'd wondered if the directions she'd been given had been wrong. But, at last, here she was.

Sara popped the boot of the car and lifted out her bags, one by one. It had taken almost a week to smuggle them out of the house. She'd used work, her grandmother, and even asked the community nurse to help.

She'd been so nervous for days, every muscle tight, her insides trembling. All it would have taken was for Greg to notice one little thing. To ask one tiny question. "Where's that jacket you always wear?" Or "Why don't you put on that dress I like?" Then her plans would have unravelled.

Her hand strayed to her belly, just for a moment, and the judgement threatened to overwhelm her. That her plans for freedom had been so fragile, that she had lived that way for so long, still ate at her soul like acid. The counsellor had told her she was brave for leaving but Sara knew different. She had only done it now because her cowardice had been shown up.

She shook off the emotion, refusing to give in to her tiredness or her tears. Not yet.

Taking the first of the bags, she made her way to the front door, the long grass scratching at her legs. Three steps led up to an old wooden veranda, then the front door. The key her grandmother had given her stuck at first. The lock was old and rusted. But at last it gave way and the door opened. Taking a deep breath, Sara stepped inside.

"This is the house where I grew up," her grandmother had told her, pressing the key into Sara's palm just a few days before. "It's not much, but it'll be a good place to hide out and get your bearings again."

Sara had felt the sharp edges of the key like a serrated knife. "I can't. I don't know anyone. I…"

The old woman shook her head. "You can. And you will. You know it's time."

The crisp rough sheets and antiseptic smell of the hospital room had mixed with the sweet fragrance of flowers in a sensory reminder of where she was and why. She lowered her hand to rest above her vacant womb. How could she stay when someone so much more helpless would not? "Yeah, I guess I do."

"Then go. He won't find you there."

The musty smell hit her like a wave as she stepped over the threshold. It was clear no one had lived here in decades. Sara had to admit her grandmother was right – no one would find her here. The locals even thought it was haunted, judging by what the woman in the store had said. Well, that was fine with Sara. She would fit right in – a ghost of her former self, haunted by her experiences.

The door led into a hallway, with a staircase at the far end. Doors opened at irregular intervals, left and right. Sara set down her bag and searched for a light switch.

There wasn't one.

"Oh, come on." She let the bag slide to the ground and checked again.

The windows let in the late afternoon sun but shadows in the house were building. She began exploring the rooms to the side of the hallway. They were of varying sizes and shapes, bedrooms, living rooms, dining room, kitchen with a large preparation surface and an ancient wood burning stove – but no fridge. Furniture was covered in dusty sheets and cobwebs were strung up like party streamers.

No light bulbs hung from the ceilings. No power sockets graced the walls.

"You've got to be kidding me. No power at all?" She felt the last of her energy sag from her body. A little voice in her mind told her she was stupid for having expected things to be easy. After all, why would the power be connected anyway when no one was living here? It was typical of the sort of stupid expectations she always had.

She knew that voice. Knew it well.

"Go home, Greg," she told it. "I don't listen to you anymore."

As if to make her a liar, her phone buzzed. She automatically pulled it out of her handbag to see who was calling.

It was him. She hit ignore and the screen flicked back to the list of missed calls and text messages.

She slid her finger over the screen and cycled through them all. She knew what they would say. She didn't need to hear it. She hovered over the screen, her resolve wavering. Perhaps she should listen. Just in case. If it was bad, well, she was far away now anyway.

She took a deep breath. Could she face listening to him right now? Did she owe it to him after their years together? After so much pain?

Just one then. To see what he knew.

Her finger dove downward but never reached the screen. To her surprise, the phone flickered and went black.

She shook it, and pressed the power button. Nothing. The battery was dead and with it the last of the electricity in the house.

Sara sighed and hurried outside to bring in the rest of her bags before the sun set completely and there was no more light.

It would be like camping, she decided. She would

make up a bed on one of the couches in the living room and explore the rest of the house later. The spaghetti she'd bought would do just as well eaten cold, and tomorrow she would go into town and buy a gas burner to last until she could get electricity connected.

In the meantime, she was fine. She was safe and she was fine.

Despite the strange creaks of the house timber and the whistling of the wind in the trees outside, Sara felt she really was safer than she'd been in a long time.

As sleep crept in to claim her, another sound reached her ears. A strange, whispery voice calling her name.

CHAPTER THREE

The sunlight that had crept into the house that morning was slow to make its presence known. The shadows made way for it only grudgingly, when the heavy but moth-eaten fabric in the windows could no longer hold it back. Sara stretched and pushed back the covers she'd draped over herself in the night – then tried not to cough as the motion stirred up clouds of dust.

Strange as it had been to sleep in this huge house all alone, she felt rested. She glanced at her watch and frowned. The hands had stopped moving. She tapped it with her finger. Nothing. The battery must need replacing. Between that and her phone being out of charge, the only indication of the time was the growling in her stomach.

A quick meal of cereal and room temperature milk sorted that, then she found the bathroom and took a cold shower. "At least there's running water," she muttered to portraits in the hall as she wandered back to the living room in nothing but a towel.

She pulled open one of her bags and then hesitated. She would need to do a lot of cleaning today to make the old house liveable – even if only in a few rooms to start with. She really ought to dress accordingly. Maybe track pants and an old t-shirt. Something she didn't mind getting dirty in.

Somehow, her fingers lingered on her favourite sundress. The green and white one that Greg hardly ever let her wear.

Sod it. She felt like being pretty. She put it on and immediately felt better. There was something about a full skirt in an old house that just seemed to fit. She was like a heroine in a black and white movie.

She clasped one hand to her breast. "Honestly, Tara, I'll never go hungry again!" She collapsed onto the sofa in fits of giggles. There was no way that was the right quote but she didn't care. For once, there was nobody here to correct her and she could do and say what she liked.

"Whatever. The. Fuck. I. Like." Each word rang louder, like a hammer striking off her chains. This was brilliant.

Today, she decided, would be all about her. A day when she would do what she liked, when she liked, and enjoy it. The question was, what did she want to do?

She sat up and looked around. She could explore the house and grounds some more. She could read. She could go back to the store and get some decent food and a camp cooker and make herself something good to eat. And find somewhere to recharge her phone so she could call her grandmother and the electrical company. She didn't know how long she was going to stay here but she knew she wouldn't want to go long without electricity.

"First things first," she told the empty house. "Chocolate."

She grabbed her handbag and headed out to the car. The key in the ignition clicked and the engine wheezed. For a moment Sara thought it had died. She checked the lights in case she'd left them on overnight – nope, they were switched off. She held her breath and turned the key again and this time the engine roared into life. She breathed out again. It was still a good day.

It wasn't until she'd parked the car in the tiny strip of shops Kowhiowhio called "town" that she remembered the awkwardness with the shopkeeper the day before. If the same woman was behind the counter well, she'd just have to brazen it out or apologise. It wasn't like there was another store to go to anywhere near. She bit her lip and tucked her hair behind her ear. There was no trace of the bruise today and it was nice to wear it back from her face.

She stepped inside the shop and sure enough, there was Moana. The woman had her dark hair up in a bun with a greenstone spike through it to hold it in place. Another piece of *pounamu* hung around her neck as a pendant. Her dark eyes narrowed a little when she saw Sara and her mouth tightened, but she said nothing.

Sara met her eyes for a moment, then turned away. "This is a day for me," she reminded herself under her breath. "Just enjoy it."

She picked up a basket and went straight for the chocolate. A large block, then a bag of pineapple lumps. "Do you stock wine?" she called. This felt like a wine day.

The Maori woman pointed silently.

Sara added a bottle of her favourite merlot, then went back and gave each aisle a thorough going over. She wanted to stock up with enough to last a few days, but not so much that it spoiled without a fridge.

She carried what she could up to the counter. Moana began to silently ring it up. Sara could feel herself getting annoyed. Sure, she had been rude to the woman yesterday, but Moana had been rude to her first. Surely a smile or a pleasant greeting wasn't too much to ask so they could start afresh?

She forced a smile on her own face. "You don't stock camp stoves, by any chance? Like a little gas cooker?"

"The hardware store up the road has them."

That was something. "Thanks." She pointed to the electrical booth at the side of the store, currently unstaffed. "What about a battery for my watch?"

Moana sighed. "Yeah, we have those." She glanced at Sara's wrist, then went across to the booth and brought back a small battery in a tiny plastic bag. "You can leave the watch here for Nate to sort out when he gets back or you can take the battery now and do it yourself."

"I can do it," Sara said. "Just add it to the rest." She paused a moment, then decided it was up to her to make peace. "Hey, I'm sorry if I was a bit short with you yesterday. It's been a rough week."

Moana nodded slowly as she scanned the rest of the items and pursed her lips. "Kia Ora," she said at last. "That's fair enough. I respect that you've come from a long way away and you don't know much about the local area. Just so you know, me and my husband have a number of roles in this community outside of this shop and one of those is being on the local marae and the city council. We're looking at having that O'Neill house condemned."

Sara felt the pleasure of the day fall away like broken glass. "What? Why?"

"Well, it's an eyesore for starters and it's falling down anyway. It's a hazard. It should be demolished."

Sara felt her nails digging into her palm. "That's not your decision though, is it? It's not your house so it's really none of your business."

"It is my business when local children go trespassing in there trying to find the ghosts and could very easily get hurt."

"Well perhaps you should concentrate on keeping your children out of other people's houses!"

Moana's eyes narrowed again. "There shouldn't be a house there anyway. That land is *tapu*."

"What?" Sara could hear her voice rising but she didn't care. "That's ridiculous. That house has been in my family, on that land, for generations. You can't just decide it's sacred now!"

Groceries were stuffed into plastic bags with steadily increasing force. "And my family has known for generations that there shouldn't be a house there. It's too close to *Rarohenga*. To the netherworld."

Sara grabbed the bags and packed the last two items herself. "Oh for fuck's sake. If you want to believe in superstition that's your business but leave my family's home alone."

This was her safe place. Her haven! She had finally

found somewhere to run to and now this busybody wanted to tear it down? She was shaking with rage as she left the shop. There had to be something she could do!

She jammed the groceries in the back seat and threw the car into reverse. This time it started immediately and the engine roared with her fury as she drove off.

A few minutes later she'd cooled down just enough to think she hadn't handled herself well. Her best bet had been to change Moana's mind from the start and she wouldn't have much chance of that now.

"You've messed up the diplomacy option," she told herself. "As always." Why did she always struggle with escalating an argument? It had been the same with Greg. One minute she'd be tiptoeing around him and the next practically picking the fight herself, knowing how it was going to end.

But at least then the tension wasn't so smothering. When it was over, he would be nice for a few days. She could relax.

Relax and convince herself things were okay again.

"You're all sass and no spine, my girl," her grandmother had told her once. "One day you'll put that fire into action and there'll be no stopping you."

Well she'd done it at last. She'd taken action and gotten to her sanctuary. There was no way anyone was taking it from her now.

"So, what's the first step?" She'd made a plan to leave Greg and carried it out. Making a plan to deal with Moana should be simple compared to that.

She'd need to sort the house out and make it presentable to an assessor – well that was easy enough, she'd been planning to tidy it up anyway. She'd need to make some phone calls to the city council and see what the criteria were for having a house condemned. She had a fairly good idea how to do that…except she didn't have a working phone.

As she turned into the gravel road, the solution struck her. The neighbours would have electricity and maybe she could get them on side about the house. She'd kill two birds with one stone and try her diplomacy after all. Perhaps she could convince the rest of the town to leave her house alone.

She pulled the car over beside the second to last house on the road, her next door neighbour. It would be good to say hello anyway, right? That was the neighbourly thing to do in a small town.

The front door was open when she approached. She raised her hand to knock and then saw a very attractive male rear bent over in the living room inside, filling out his jeans very nicely indeed. The day was looking up again!

He was talking to a cage on the floor with a kitten inside. "Come on, little guy. It's okay. Be quiet."

Sara let a grin play on her face. Sexy men and kittens. Clearly someone wanted to cheer her up.

Then he stood up and turned around. It was the man from the store. Moana's husband.

CHAPTER FOUR

Nate Adams set down the cage in his living room and the creature inside howled piteously. Nate wondered how so much sound could come from such a tiny ball of fur. His stomach tensed for a moment. He hoped he'd made the right decision. If this went wrong, he would never hear the end of it from Moana.

She had a real thing for sticking with an issue once she got hold of it. For about six months now she'd been serving peas at every family meal and insisting Abigail eat them, despite knowing full well they were the only vegetable the poor girl refused to eat. It was incredibly frustrating and unnecessary to Nate's mind, but she kept doing it, as if determined to take on more and more of a parent role for Abigail.

Ever since Emma had died, Moana had gotten more and more opinionated about his parenting. It wasn't that he didn't appreciate advice – he was the first to admit that the prospect of raising a daughter on his own had scared the crap out of him – but under the circumstances, he thought he was doing okay. Extended family support was one thing, interference and undermining was another. Explaining the difference to his sister-in-law was no easy task.

Yesterday, at the store, had been one of the few times he'd ever seen Moana at a loss for words – and that had been due to his new neighbour. She might have been a slip of a city girl, but she'd put Mo in her place quickly enough. He might have to take lessons on her style!

He went back to the car and brought in the bag of cat food and kitty litter, nudging the door open with his foot as he did so. He put them down on the kitchen bench, then stuck the ribbon he'd bought on top of the bag of litter. The irony of the placement made him chuckle.

He could just imagine Abi's face when she saw it and realised what it meant.

Responsibility for Abigail was a topic they'd been debating for a while. Mo thought he spoiled Abi. Perhaps he did a little. It was hard not to when they were all each other had. But this was an idea he'd come to on his own and he was sure it would help. Giving Abi responsibility for a pet would help her learn the importance of her actions and give her a furry friend as well.

The kitchen was part of the open plan living space of the house, with a bench lined with stools separating it from the lounge area. It was where he and Abigail ate breakfast together, so that the used cereal bowls could be pushed quickly into the sink as they rushed to get ready for work and school, rather than at the dining table, just a few steps further away. This morning's bowls were still there, and he ran a little water into them to soften any cereal left behind so he could wash up before Abi got home.

The kitten watched him with wide eyes and continued yowling.

"Come on, little guy," he soothed, walking back into the lounge room and poking his fingers through the cage bars for the tiny creature to sniff. "Just stay put until Abi gets home from school, okay? Not long now."

An amused female voice came from the doorway behind him. "Do you usually get good results negotiating with animals?"

Nate chuckled. "You'd be surprised."

He straightened up and turned to see the town newcomer on his doorstep. Her dark, almost black hair was tucked behind her ears in thick waves that contrasted with her pale skin. Yesterday, he'd thought her eyes were dark blue, but now he realised they were green. They matched the pattern on the sundress she was wearing. There was something more relaxed in her face today, and in her bearing. She was as striking to look at as she had been to talk to at the shop yesterday. He supposed the neighbourly thing to do would have been to go over to the O'Neill house with some baking this morning, but his baking was hardly welcoming and now it seemed she'd beaten him to it.

When she saw his face, however, her eyes widened and her face turned red. "Oh. You're the guy from the shop."

He smiled and held out his hand. "Yeah. Nate Adams. Good to meet you properly since we're neighbours."

She awkwardly stepped forward to shake it. "Sara O'Neill." She scrunched up her nose. "I…um…I'm sorry if I was rude yesterday. It was a long drive…"

"No worries," he said, and meant it. He felt his smile get wider at the memory. "Moana can have that effect on people. O'Neill? So it's your family's house? Did you find it okay?"

She nodded. "Yeah, your directions were great. It's…a bit rustic, but I found it easily enough."

Nate laughed. "Rustic. Yeah, that's one word for it. I'm surprised it hasn't been condemned."

Her jaw tensed and he noticed what looked like the remnants of a faded bruise on the side of her cheek. "Actually, it seems structurally stable. It just needs some work and…I don't think it's very fair of you to try to have someone else's home condemned."

Nate blinked. "What? I'm not. I just meant it's been abandoned for a long time."

"Your wife said you were."

"Um…" It was a punch in the gut, even after this long. "My wife has been dead for about three years. I think you have me confused with someone else."

Her mouth worked silently for a moment, like a startled fish. "Oh God. I'm so sorry! I thought you and Moana…"

He let out a bark of laughter. "God, no! She was my wife's sister, that's all. My daughter's aunt."

"Oh." Her face was even redder now than it had been when she'd first recognised him.

He took pity. "Easy mistake to make. No harm done. Did you come over for anything in particular?"

"Um, actually, yes." She held up her cellphone and

charger. "The house doesn't have any electricity yet. Would it be okay if I plug this in here for a bit? I need to call my grandmother and let her know I'm okay."

"Sure." Nate pointed to the wall. "There's a socket over there. I'll make us a coffee while you wait." He put the electric kettle on and took two mugs out of the cupboard. "So you sound like you know a bit about the house. Have you been out here before?"

Sara plugged in the phone charger and shrugged. "Actually, my grandmother only told me about it a week ago. She grew up there. I don't think anyone's lived in it since."

"I'm guessing it was in better condition back then," Nate said.

She chuckled. "Yeah. I'd hope so. But that's okay. My partner and I…" She frowned. "Ex-partner…we did a bit of renovating houses. So I'm used to living in a state of disrepair."

Nate carefully ignored her correction. "Are you planning to renovate here?" He got the milk out of the fridge and put it on the bench next to the coffee mugs.

Sara took it and poured a little into one of the cups, then settled on one of the stools that lined the other side of the bench. "I hadn't really thought about it until today, but it would give me something to do while I'm here. At the very least I need to get the electricity sorted and make whatever repairs are needed to stop your sister-in-law knocking the place down."

That seemed reasonable. "I can lend you a generator if you like. Just to get you going."

She shook her head. "Thanks, but letting me charge my phone is help enough. I'll call and get the power company to hook me up."

"Fair enough."

The coffee was ready and they both took a sip. The rich flavour spilled over Nate's tongue, soothing and warm. The smell of it was invigorating. Sara seemed to be enjoying her cup just as much. Nate wondered if the lack of electricity over at the old house extended to a lack of kitchen facilities. If so, she'd likely not had any coffee since sometime yesterday. Too long for any decent human.

Speaking of decent, he was suddenly aware of the ribboned bag of kitty litter on the bench. Hardly the hallmark of a good and gentlemanly host. But then she'd already seen the kitten so hopefully she would understand.

The suspiciously quiet kitten.

His stomach suddenly in knots, Nate leaned over the bench, peering past Sara into the living room. The door of the cage was open. The kitten was gone.

His coffee mug hit the bench with a thud. "Damn it!"

He noticed Sara jump and felt a stab of guilt at startling her. He must have banged the cup louder than he'd thought.

"What is it?" she said, gripping her own cup tight like a safety line. Or a weapon.

Nate sighed. "The kitten I bought for my daughter has escaped. Is the front door still open?"

She glanced sideways to check. "Yes, sorry."

He shrugged. "Not your fault. I thought the cage was secure. Damn. I hope he hasn't gone far."

Sara frowned, her mouth open as if she'd expected

to have to argue the matter.

Nate wondered what her ex had been like if she felt the need to justify her lack of blame for a random occurrence. "Can you check in there? I'll see if I can spot him in the yard."

He hurried out the door and looked over the yard. No sign of the kitten. He got on his hands and knees and looked under Sara's car and his own. Still nothing.

What if the little ball of fur had gotten under the house? Or wandered across the road into the bushes? He might never be found and starve to death instead of living the pampered life of a loved pet Nate had intended. Not to mention how disappointed Abigail would be and how Moana would lord it over him.

He stood up and turned in a slow circle, eyes searching every nook and shadow, ears straining for the slightest sound. "Puss?" he called softly. "Come on kitty. Come back. I'll get you some food."

A shriek came from inside the house. Nate was already running when the sound was followed by laughter. He jumped the front steps and stood in the doorway.

Sara stood in the middle of the room, her hips swaying gently, letting the full skirt of her dress flare just a touch. About half way up the skirt, claws clinging to the fabric as he made his way higher, was the kitten.

Sara's laugh was infectious. As she reached for the kitten, he scurried sideways across her skirt. "Help! Apparently he thinks I'm a tree!"

Nate quickly closed the door behind him and hurried forward. He made a grab for the kitten but it dodged him and scurried higher up Sara's dress and around her waist to the small of her back.

"Ow! God, he's got sharp little claws!" She turned to keep Nate facing the kitten.

Before Nate could catch him, however, the little furball had reached her shoulder and stopped, burying its face in her neck.

Nate chuckled. "I think you have a friend."

Sara cooed and smiled. "You might not say that if it was your body he used as a jungle gym. He is adorable though." She reached up and gave the kitten a little scratch behind the ears. He purred loud as a tractor.

"How did you find him?"

"He found me." She sniffed slightly. "Cats always seem to find me. I swear they know I'm allergic."

"You're allergic?" Nate hurried forward to pluck the kitten from her shoulder. The little black and white bundle gave a little mew of protest but stayed settled.

"It's fine." Sara moved back across to the kitchen bench and took a sip out of her discarded coffee. "I'll sniff and sneeze a bit but it doesn't get any worse than that." She watched as he put the kitten back in its cage and shut the door firmly. "You said this little guy is for your daughter?"

"Yeah." Nate straightened up and went back to his own coffee. It was luke warm, but she continued to drink hers so he did the same. "She's seven and I wanted something to try to teach her some responsibility."

Sara glanced at the bag of kitty litter with the bow attached. "Okay. So she gets a kitten but all the chores that go with it – responsibility with consequences for a creature she loves and can have empathy for."

Nate blinked. “Yeah. That’s the idea. Although I wouldn’t have put it quite like that.”

Sara chuckled and pointed to herself. “Early childhood teacher. We get trained to think about things like that.”

“Oh.” It made sense, Nate thought. She seemed like she’d be good with kids. “So you think it’s a good idea? I…don’t always know what I’m doing. I’m raising her on my own these days.”

She shrugged. “Depends on the child. But it’s not a bad one. Just make sure she’s capable of the tasks you set her and has a good understanding of what’s expected and the consequences for both her and the kitten if she doesn’t do it. And make them consequences you can actually follow through on. You don’t want to threaten something and then not be able to carry it out.” She nodded in the direction of the cage. “Like threatening to get rid of this little guy when in a day you’ll be too in love with him to truly consider it.”

Nate snorted. “You really think it’ll take a whole day?”

“Good point! I’m guessing you’re there already.”

“God, when I saw him climbing up your dress like that…” They both chuckled into their coffee mugs. “Abigail is going to love him.”

Sara nodded. “I’m sure she will.”

How was it he could talk so easily about raising Abi with this near stranger when it was so difficult with his wife’s sister? He watched her with interest. This was a woman more interesting than any he’d met in a long time. To be honest, he hadn’t been this comfortable talking about Abi with anyone since Em had died.

“Do you have children of your own?” he asked.

The light dropped out of Sara’s eyes. She stared into her coffee cup. “No. No, that’s not for me, I’m afraid.” She set the cup down and stood up. “I’m sure my phone will have enough charge by now. Thank you for the coffee. Sorry to have taken up your time.”

Nate stood as well, confused. “That’s okay. Stay a bit longer if you want…”

But she’d already unplugged her phone charger and was wrapping the cord around the phone on her way to the door. “Thanks again. Tell Moana I’ll have the house ready for her assessment very soon. She’s not getting a chance to knock it down.”

And with that, she was gone. Leaving Nate intrigued and wondering exactly what had gone wrong.

CHAPTER FIVE

The man from the power company arrived early in the morning, two days later. He was a portly, balding man with a round friendly face and blue overalls with the logo of a running man holding a bolt of lightning stitched on the front. He introduced himself as Edward, circled the house from the outside, then asked if there was access to either the ceiling or underneath the house.

Sara had to admit she didn't know about either.

In the few days she'd been living here, she'd cleaned, dusted and aired out every room she could find in what had turned out to be the most bewilderingly designed house she'd ever stayed in. The layout was almost as if three or four houses had been squashed together like warm marshmallows, blending and sticking until the seams melded together and the resultant shape made no sense. It twisted and turned back in on itself, one room leading to another, hallways ending in blank walls. At the back of the house was a conservatory filled with wicker furniture that overlooked a strange mix of orchard and native bush, as though the colonial influence of the fruit trees had somehow been absorbed into the punga and totara forest.

The floors were covered in threadbare carpets in some areas, and polished wood in others – some of which she would have sworn were kauri, which, if true, would have been worth a huge amount. The warm golden glow of it was a comfort somehow, despite the tendency of the old house to creak and groan alarmingly while she was alone in the dark at night.

She'd chosen a bedroom for herself the first day – no more sleeping on the couch for her. A huge, four-poster bed dominated the room and the romance of it called to her despite the sagging mattress. It'd taken her a good part of an hour to drag a second mattress from another room and drop it on the first before the bed was comfortable enough to sleep on. It raised her very high above the floor and she felt like the princess and the pea, as she drifted off that night. Even more so when she added a candle and matches to the old style writing desk in the corner. She might as well have been a Jane Austen heroine in some grand, gothic tale.

"Well, I wouldn't have believed it, but you're right," Edward said as he climbed down out of the attic. "I can't find any original wiring at all. I've lost a bet back at the office."

Sara chuckled. "Sorry about that. It's as strange to me as it is to you! I can't believe nobody thought to wire up the place before now. Have you ever seen a house without electricity before?"

He shook his head. "Can't say I have. I can connect you to the grid today and install a meter box, but you'll need to get a local electrician in to wire up the place for lights and wall sockets. Not to mention hot water." He shook his head again.

Sara bit her lip. "Could you put in at least one wall socket before you go? It could be a while before I can get anyone else out here."

He looked her up and down. "Missing your TV shows, are you?"

"Hot food, mostly."

He grunted. "Fair enough. I'll see what I can do if I have time."

"Thanks." The only local electrician Sara knew of was Nate Adams – and she wasn't ready to go to him for help again after the debacle she'd made of herself last time.

She had to admit, he'd been friendly enough. And he certainly was quite easy on the eyes. With his dark brown hair, very slightly too long, curled down over his forehead, muscular arms and broad chest filling out his t-shirt, he'd made an impression. Unfortunately, she suspected she'd made an impression too – the wrong kind!

She cringed inwardly as the power company man brought in his bundles of cable and the fuse box. The look on Nate's face when she'd launched into him for wanting to condemn her house – and all because she'd made the stupid assumption that he and Moana were married. She should have known a man who had been nothing but helpful wouldn't be paired with that trouble maker.

She left Edward to his work and wandered the rest of the house, making mental notes of the work that needed to be done. Where the priorities were for wiring needs, what walls or floorboards looked like they might need replacing, where the ceiling was discoloured, suggesting a leak in the roof.

Try as she might to focus on the tasks at hand, her mind wandered back to Nate Adams. At least she'd managed to make herself seem intelligent for a few brief moments before running from the house like some emotionally damaged Cinderella at midnight.

She sighed. Why did he have to ask her about children?

Even now, her hand strayed to her stomach. It was stupid, but she couldn't help doing it. The child that had been there was gone. A little girl, they'd told her.

She took a deep, steadying breath, and pulled her hands back to her sides, fingers curled into fists so tight her nails dug into her palms. The pain felt good. She deserved it. This was not the time to be thinking about a man. Her weakness with a man was what had caused all her trouble.

Her weakness over Greg.

She'd only been in art school a year when the handsome young man had swept her off her feet. He'd come to an exhibition one of her friends had been a part of and they'd spent the entire evening chatting in the corner. He made her laugh and he thought she was an artist until she'd admitted none of the work was her own. He'd told her she looked the part and that it suited her and asked her to coffee. Then, when an argument with her mother led to her deciding she needed a place of her own, he came to the rescue with a spare room at his flat and he helped her move.

It'd been an organic, wonderful relationship after that. They would make love in the mornings, he would go to work and she would study, draw and paint, then they'd spend their evenings together talking about the world and its problems, and solve them over a glass of red wine.

It was one such evening that they'd hit on the plan for their future.

"We have the tools," Greg said. "We could really set things up for ourselves. I have some money saved up and you've got the design talent. What if we buy old houses and do them up together for a profit?"

It had seemed like a good idea at the time. A bit of work but something they could be doing together and the outcome would give them a future their friends wouldn't have. It was a good plan.

Sara shook her head wryly thinking about it. That first house had been a disaster. Almost as run down as this place and much less structurally sound. They hadn't known what they were doing and it was a harsh life lesson to learn on the job. They'd paid far too much for tradesmen to do things they could have done themselves and tried to do things themselves they'd have been better to hire professionals for. They had to jib and plaster twice to make up for their lack of skill the first time and the budget blew way out of control.

It was hard not to see it as her own fault. Greg had to continue with his day job to bring in the finances – her student debt and meagre part time work did very little to keep them afloat. Her job was to ensure the house was aesthetically pleasing enough to sell for a good price at the end of it. She also had the time during the day to make sure things got done. She began skipping classes to keep an eye on the tradesmen and to keep up with Greg's expectations for how quickly the work would be done.

"I can't keep us afloat like this forever," he told her. "And it's not like you're going to be much help getting us out of debt with an art career. You're not exactly Picasso."

Sadly, that was true. Her grades diving, Sara eventually admitted the truth and changed degrees. Her early childhood education qualification could be done partly by correspondence and she was able to work part time in a local day-care centre to gain credit as well as pay. But it wasn't enough.

The house sold at a loss. And that night Greg hit her for the first time.

She couldn't blame him. The emotional and financial stress had been unbearable and they'd both made the mistake of drowning their misery with alcohol. She remembered the look of horror on his face the second he realised what he'd done. That expression stung her much more than the pain in her cheek.

"Oh God, I'm so sorry! I didn't mean it!"

She stroked his arm and soothed him, testing her jaw. No real harm done. "It's okay, babe. It's fine. Just…settle down, okay?"

He nodded, his face crumpled into tears. Actual tears. She'd never seen him cry before, no matter what had gone wrong with the house. "I'm sorry. I just…lost it for a moment. God, are you all right?"

She forced a smile even though it hurt. "Yeah, I'm fine. It's been a hard day. Don't worry about it. Let's forget it ever happened."

He reached out and gently traced along her cheek. "I will never do that again, Sara. I promise. I just…"

She nodded. "I know."

"God, what do we do now?"

She made her voice gentle, soothing, like she would for the kids. Full of hope. "Well, we've learned heaps, haven't we? It would be a pity to waste that."

He tilted his head and looked at her. "You think we should try again? You'd do that?"

She'd never be able to pay him back for the money he'd lost on this venture if they didn't. "Of course. We won't make the same mistakes this time. We know what we're doing. We chalk this one up to experience and we go from here. Next time we spend less and we sell for more. But no more hitting! Deal?"

He gave that boyish, rueful smile that melted her heart. "Yeah. I promise. Never again."

As Sara stepped out into one of the halls of the big old O'Neill house, she wondered if she were even the same woman any more. Greg wasn't the same man…yet, horribly, there were glimpses still. Her heart ached, not for the man she had left behind, but the man who had somehow faded from their relationship so long ago, whose body and mannerisms had been inhabited by…something new.

Sara sighed. Hardly new. She had to face that. She'd been hiding from it for far too long.

She looked up and the old sepia toned portrait on the wall looked back. A stern woman with her hair up in a bun and a blouse buttoned tight up her throat with a broach locking it in place. On her lap sat a huge tabby cat, proud as an Egyptian goddess. The woman stroked the cat with a hand weighed down by an enormous gemstoned ring.

"You wouldn't let a man mess you around, would you?" Sara asked the portrait. "You're far too sensible for that." For a moment, she could have sworn the woman in the old photograph winked and she chuckled at her own imagination. "Us girls have to stick together, sister."

As she turned away, a voice whispered, "Yesss."

"What?" Sara spun around but the hallway was empty. Nothing but shadows, old furniture and framed portraits looked back at her. "Who's there?"

A scream came from the front of the house.

Sara ran for the exit. Her chest felt as though she'd swallowed acid, her lungs tight with panic. For a moment, she forgot the way out and opened the wrong door. Shelves of musty linen blocked her path and she stared at them in shock before realising what she'd done. She slammed the cupboard closed and grabbed the next door handle instead, at last finding her way to the lounge and then out onto the porch.

The sun blinded her for a few seconds as she gasped in lungsful of fresh air, still uncertain of what had happened. As her eyes adjusted and her heart rate lowered, she became aware of a buzzing sound coming from the ground below the porch. She leaned over the rail and looked down.

Edward lay beneath a tangle of cable, his body thrashing against the ground. Sparks of electricity danced around his overalls, seeming to bring the lightning bolt monogram to harsh, shocking life. A ladder lay across his stomach, pinning him and the live cable together as the current passed through his body in a rush to reach the earth.

"Shit!" Sara took the steps two at a time, instinctively trying to get to the injured man and pull him away from the wires. But as her feet touched the ground, the world whirled around her as though she'd stepped onto a merry-go-round. Dizziness overwhelmed her and her vision blurred, morphing the garden into a photographic negative of the portrait in the hall. She thought she heard the voice again. "Stay back!"

Sara pulled herself back to the solid wooden boards of the porch and the feeling passed.

Electricity. What did she remember about dealing with electricity? It was dangerous and the longer she left Edward laying there, the worse it would be for him but if she got too close and there was no one else to help... She grabbed her phone and dialled 111, requesting an ambulance in short, tense sentences.

The operator tried to keep her calm. "Stay clear of the wires, ma'am. You'll only hurt yourself if you get close. Do you know where to switch the power off at the mains?"

"No." There wasn't a main circuit board installed yet! Edward had to have tapped into the supply from the street. Surely he would have had the company turn it off first?

"The ambulance is on its way. They'll be there soon."

Sara could see the edges of Edward's overalls beginning to singe and melt. "Not soon enough."

She put the phone down and took a deep breath.

This had to be fast.

She ran down the stairs and leapt toward the dying man, pushing with all her might at the ladder and its deadly tangle of live wire. The force of electricity hit her like an angry slap and the world went grey.

CHAPTER SIX

"I told you so." Moana shook her head and tutted. "I warned you that house was a place of spirits and *ira atua*."

Sara dropped her basket of supplies on the counter with a thud. Her entire body ached with the aftermath of the shock she'd received saving the man from the power company and the paramedics had said she was lucky to be alive. Poor Edward had not been nearly so fortunate. Burns had covered much of his body and they'd still been working on him when they helicoptered him away. It seemed unlikely he or anyone else would be hooking her house up to the grid in a hurry.

"It wasn't spirits, Moana," she told the woman. "It was a silly mistake." Someone hadn't disconnected the main line before he'd tapped into it. Or had switched it back on before he was done. Or something. It hurt to even think about it.

"It's a dangerous house," Moana said.

Sara sighed. "Well, you should be happy I'm renovating it then. It won't be dangerous and it won't be an eyesore. So you can relax."

Moana handed her the bag of groceries. "We'll have to see about that. The council building assessor is coming next month. And nobody in this town will work on that house. Nobody."

When she arrived home, Sara stared at the scorch marks on the grass. Moana's words echoed in her mind. Somehow they morphed in her memory, turning and deepening. "Nobody will work on your house. Nobody will want your work. Nobody will want you if I leave. You're nothing." Greg's voice.

She sat on the steps and something inside her trembled. The wood was warm and smooth to the touch and the smell of burnt dirt was still strong even now. It filled her lungs. It was a scent of death.

She felt the tightness in her chest rise and spill into her throat. "Stupid. So stupid." Why must she always be so close to death? Why did it have to happen again so soon?

She pressed her hands over her mouth and choked back the emotions. No, she told herself. She would not let this overwhelm her again. She rummaged in her handbag for a tissue or a distraction and found her phone. The battery was low yet again. Her e-book reader had shorted out the day before as well. Nothing electrical seemed to work in this damn house!

There were a few new messages on the screen. Her eyes slid over Greg's repeated number and paused on another. The one she could rely on. Her finger punched the screen.

"Nana?"

She could picture the old woman's kind face and

smiling brown eyes, faded now to almost hazel, in their cradle of laugh-lines. "Sara, my favourite granddaughter."

"Your only granddaughter." The familiar exchange soothed the tightness in her chest. She swallowed. "How's things?"

"Can't complain. They look after us pretty well. You know how it is."

Sara tried to smile, but her mouth wouldn't keep the shape. "Yeah, Nana. I know. That's good. Anything exciting happening?"

The old woman snorted. "Did that no good ratbag come to see me, you mean? Yes he did. But the nurses sent him on his way quick smart. They don't make us put up with the likes of him in this place, you know."

A chuckle found its way from Sara's lips despite herself. She could just imagine the stocky, no-nonsense nurse manager of the rest home evicting Greg if she considered him improper. "Good. That's good."

"Don't you worry about him. There's no way he can find you up there. You're safe and sound. Now, how are you feeling? Are you still cramping at all?"

Sara opened her mouth to tell her what had been happening, but then closed it again. As understanding as her Nana was, she didn't need to burden the old woman with yet more worry. She considered the ache in her body – at least it wasn't the familiar one from the last couple of weeks. "No. It's gone."

"You'll be okay, my girl. I know it's hard. All the women in our family have had miscarriages. The pain will fade in time."

"In the second trimester, though, Nana? Not like

this." She closed her eyes and could see the tiny form of her daughter, far too small to survive, as clearly as if there were a lightbulb inside that miniscule body. Translucent skin, doll-like hands and feet, and a thin, trembling cord that could no longer sustain her life.

"No. Not like that." The old woman's voice was soft. "There was nothing you could do."

Sara sniffed back the tears that teetered at the edge of her eyelids. "I guess." But she knew it wasn't true. Her child had known better than to come into the world Sara had created for her. This tiny unborn girl had more spine and determination than her mother had been able to muster in ten years of abuse. She had left. And in doing so, shown Sara the way. Her daughter would rather die than stay with a man who would hit her. It had been the realisation Sara needed to make her own escape. A sacrifice she was determined would not be in vain.

"Let's talk about something more cheerful," her Nana said. "How are things going up there? Are you enjoying the weather?"

Sara shook her head at the clumsy shift of topic, but latched onto it gratefully. Anything to dull the ache of guilt. "The weather's great. Really warm." She took a breath. "Hey, I've been meaning to ask you, is there any strange history to the house?"

There was a long silence. Long enough that she thought the phone battery must have cut out. "Why do you ask?" her Nana said.

Sara frowned. "A couple of people have made comments in town." She hesitated, not wanting to worry the old woman, but decided to carry on. "One of the locals wants to have the place demolished. You don't mind if I do some renovations, do you?"

"Does it need them?"

"Well, it's a bit run down." Sara picked at a flake of paint on the porch rail. "And it doesn't have electricity."

"Ah yes." Sara could hear the familiar click as her Nana sucked on her dentures and repositioned them as she thought. "It was never supposed to have electricity, you see."

"What?"

"It was part of the conditions of the original Will."

"Are you serious? Why?"

"I don't know. It was Great Great Great Aunt Bridget, who said it. She was a weird one. Never married. Apparently there was an engagement that fell through and she was never quite the same. There were all kinds of rumours. Some people said she was a witch but I think she was just a crazy old lady with cats."

Sara leaned back and stared at the porch overhang. "And she had a thing against electricity?"

"Apparently so. The house was to stay in the family, never be sold, and never go electric. The neighbourhood kids used to say she haunted the place to make sure of it. I never saw her though in all the years I lived there."

"So…are we supposed to stick to this now?" Sara rubbed a hand over her forehead. How could she explain to a building inspector that an ancestor's ghost didn't want her to put in household basics?

Nana chuckled. "No, I shouldn't think so. The house is in a trust and I've made you the main trustee. You do what you see fit, my girl. I'm glad you're keeping yourself busy."

Sara sighed in relief. "So am I, Nana. So am I."

The phone crackled in her ear, hissing static like scrunching paper.

"Hello? Nana?"

A strange voice answered. "Where are you? Come back."

Sara sat up, a jolt of cold stabbing through her like lightning. Her mind jumped to the voice she'd heard in the hallway, before Edward's scream. She'd forgotten it in amongst the drama. "Hello? Who's there? Nana?" She pulled the phone away from her ear and stared at it. The screen flickered and went black.

"Come here. Come *here*." The voice wasn't from the phone. It came from around the side of the house.

Sara put down the dead cell-phone and got to her feet. She kicked off her shoes and slowly made her way along the porch, her hand trailing lightly over the rail, as if to prove to herself that the world was solid. The smell of grass, warm wood, and wildflowers seemed somehow unreal as she suddenly realised how alone she truly was in this ancient, empty house.

Without meaning to, she found herself chanting under her breath. "It's not Greg. It's not Greg. It's not Greg." The voice was too high and there was no way he could know where she was. But somehow the words had sparked her fear response anyway.

Ira atua, Moana had said. Supernatural beings. Even her Nana had mentioned a ghost.

Sara caught her bottom lip in her teeth to stop the chant. She knew it was ridiculous – of course it was. The most likely explanation was that she'd imagined it or the phone had somehow picked up another conversation as the battery went flat. But…what if she wasn't entirely alone after all?

She reached the end of the porch and, taking a deep breath, leaned out over the rail to look around the side of the house.

There was a yowl and something sprang out of the long grass and barrelled into her chest.

Sara screamed.

The voice shouted, "No, come back!"

Sara grabbed at the thing on her chest and her fingers touched fur. The tension drained away as she held out a familiar black and white kitten.

"You! God, you gave me a fright."

A little girl of about six or seven came running around the corner. She had black hair, coffee coloured skin and wide, dark eyes. "Oscar! Come *back*, you bad kitten." She skidded to a halt when she saw Sara, her mouth open in a perfect O.

Sara couldn't help but laugh, grateful that here was an actual flesh and blood person after all her foolish fears about ghosts. "You must be Abigail. I'm Sara. I've met your dad and Oscar before."

The kitten, held out at arm's length with his back feet dangling, began to purr loudly.

Abigail blinked. "You have?"

"The day your dad got you Oscar, here."

The girl shrugged. "He ran away. Do you live here now?"

Sara nodded. "I do."

"That's good. The other lady was lonely."

Sara felt her stomach tighten but she kept a smile on

her face. "What other lady?"

Abigail shrugged again. "I dunno. Can I have my kitten back?"

"Of course." Sara crouched down and thrust the kitten through the porch railings to where Abigail could take it.

The little girl hugged the kitten to her and Sara half expected it to scramble away again, but instead the little cat seemed to have settled. "Okay, I'm going home now."

"Okay. Walk carefully."

"I will." Abigail strode off towards the gravel road, wading through the long grass like water. When she reached the gate, she paused, and turned back. "My daddy can help you with your house. He makes electricity."

Sara thought about the way she'd felt when they'd been talking the other day, before she'd made a complete fool of herself. "That he does," she murmured. "That he does."

CHAPTER SEVEN

The mantle over the fireplace was carved into a design of vines. It was intricate work, each twist of vine and curl of leaf was original, clearly done by hand rather than cast from a mould and repeated. Sara had found the same motif throughout the house, growing like an organic glue, binding the various parts of the house together. Skirting boards here, door frames there, along the edge of cupboards or window frames. In what seemed to be the oldest part of the house and again in the newer, add-on sections. The vines held the house together aesthetically, binding it to nature inside and out.

Sara dipped her brush into the paint and ran it along the side of a leaf, creating shadow in the pattern, a dark line that sharpened the edge. In the back of her awareness, there was a faint crackling noise, like the build up of static charge from freshly dried laundry.

Greg leaned over her shoulder. "You've fucked that up again," he said. "It's just as well you left art school. You'd never have been any good at it."

Sara frowned. "It's just the base coat. When I put

the other colours over the top and do some blending it will look really good. Trust me."

"Trust you?" Greg sneered. "That's a laugh. After all the money you've cost me over the years with your fuck ups." He handed her a cloth. "Wipe it off and start again."

"Greg, please just be patient. I know what I'm doing." She tried to make her tone gentle.

He shook the cloth at her. "Wipe it."

"Just wait." She quickly dipped the brush into another colour to demonstrate the blend. "Let me show you…"

His hand closed around her throat and pushed her back. "What did I just tell you?"

The pain in her throat was unbearable. Worse was the fear as sparks danced in front of her eyes and she realised she couldn't breathe. "Greg, please!" She struggled to gasp out the words. The wall was hard against her back. There was nowhere to go. The light dimmed as her brain struggled to stay conscious. The sparks in her vision took on the quality of exploding fireworks, each one burning her skin as they touched. "Please!"

Something huge pushed past her cheek, raking at the hand at her throat.

Greg yelped and let go, staggering back as he cradled his hand to his chest.

A massive tabby cat jumped down from the mantle. "Us girls stick together," it said.

Sara felt her knees give way beneath her and she let herself slide down the wall onto the hard, kauri floor.

The sparks were still there – not flecks in her vision

as she'd thought, but actual sparks, coming from Greg's skin. They pooled and shimmered along his arm, melting into him. They spilled from his eyes and across his face. His glare burned yellow fire. His clothes singed to ash and drifted away, his body nothing but electricity. He opened his mouth and his tongue flicked flame. "I will have her," he said.

The tabby cat sat up straight and wrapped its tail around itself. A moment later it was not a cat at all, but the woman from the photograph in the hall, Bridget. She stood between the creature of lightning and Sara. "No," she said. "You will not." She thrust out her hand and the world exploded.

Sara sat bolt upright in the four post bed, shocked awake and gasping for breath. She'd had dreams about Greg before but this…this was something new.

She fumbled on the side table for the lighter. She'd given up on torches – the batteries died too quickly. She flicked it until the tiny flame appeared, the glow a warm light in the darkness. She held it tight until her breathing slowed and then let it die, slumping back against the pillow.

A dream. It was just a dream. She was alone in the house. Greg would never find her. She was a long way from being ready to paint the interior yet – even the beautiful vine carvings that she'd vowed to preserve in her renovations. The dream was just her fears coming back to play with her subconscious mind. Ghosts and electrocutions, Greg and her lost baby – was it any wonder she would be having nightmares?

She lay for a long time in the darkness, aware that her nightgown was wet with sweat. There was no way she could sleep again now. She might as well get up.

She scuffed her feet across the floor slowly, moving toward the window. When she tugged at the fabric, pale gold light spilled through the glass. It was almost dawn.

She picked up a robe and wrapped it around herself before heading outside. The cool, crisp air was a balm for her troubled thoughts. She watched the top of the sun peek over the horizon, then stepped into the long, dew-covered grass. Being so focussed on the house, she hadn't explored the grounds much since she'd gotten here. Now was as good a time as any.

The back of the house was in worse shape than the front. Several of the wooden boards had come loose and there were signs of animals using the gaps to nest in. Weeds grew even higher here and wild native bush blended with ancient, moss-covered fruit trees in a mess of vegetation. The leaves were damp and, even in the dawn light, shadow painted each step with interesting depth and mystery.

Sara remembered the paint bush in her dream – her attempt to capture natural shading in the carved motif in the house. Nature's light did so much more than she ever could. Even a confident, capable, dream-self. The part of her that always appreciated beauty, always looked for ways to create it, was entranced.

As she watched, light pooled in pockets amongst the shadows. It lit up patches of mist that drifted between the trees like will-o'-the-wisps in a fairy-tale. They circled each other, dancing like elves in moonlight, then slowly glided deeper into the bush.

Entranced, Sara followed.

The world had a hazy, dream-like quality this early

in the morning. The breeze was soft and each touch of grass or leaf or branch was like a caress on her skin. She wandered for several minutes, following the trails of light and shadow, while birds made music around her.

Punga, tea tree and kowhai finally gave way to a clearing of moss and wildflowers. The misty lights swirled around the clearing and then sank downward, disappearing from sight.

As she came closer, Sara saw there was a pool of water in the clearing, perfectly round, with a tree at each point of the compass around its edge and large flat stones set between the trees. In the centre of the pool, something raised up to break free of the water. For a moment, Sara thought it was a doorway. She looked again and saw it was a small tree, twisted and misshapen by the elements.

Beneath the surface of the water, the dawn was splintered into little butterflies of light flitting back and forth. They called to her and she hurried forward, ready to follow them into the water.

As her toes reached the pool's edge, a cat yowled.

She stopped and shook her head. "Oscar?" she called. "Is that you again?" Surely Abigail's kitten couldn't have escaped her again already?

She looked around but couldn't see him anywhere. Somehow the image of the large tabby cat in her dream popped into her mind.

She chuckled at herself. What was she thinking? Wandering around the bush barefoot, about to step into some random pond? "Probably eels in there."

She called again for Oscar, but when no cat appeared, she walked slowly back to the house, deep in thought.

For all she'd experienced lately, there really was still beauty in the world. Those little glowing butterflies – or glow worms or whatever they were – had inspired the part of her she'd thought lost: her creativity.

She had to let go of the messages she'd let Greg infuse her with for so long. That he would mock her art skills even in her dreams was ridiculous. She had actually done very well at art school. Before she'd given up completely, some of her pieces had exhibited and actually sold, for God's sake! Art had always been something that gave her joy and she'd allowed herself to lose that joy.

Well fuck that! She was alone now and starting a new life. She would do art again.

By the time she reached the house, it was with a smile on her face.

In the bush, the waters of the pool bubbled and stirred.

CHAPTER EIGHT

When she reached the house, Sara found several vehicles parked in the gravel driveway, end to end like a metallic snake or a police road block. There was a small red Toyota, a white sedan with the city council logo on the door, and a ute with what looked like a large engine on the back of it. A group of people were arguing on the over grown lawn. They fell silent when she came towards them.

There were two men she didn't recognise, one in a pair of overalls and the other a suit, both wearing hardhats as though they were on a construction site. Next to them, her expression smugly righteous, was Moana, her back stiff and arms folded. Nate Adams stood a few paces from the other three. He spread his hands as though unconcerned, but Sara could see the tension in his strong jawline.

"I wasn't expecting visitors," she said, suddenly very conscious of her bare feet and dressing gown.

Moana's arms tightened across her chest. "Building inspection."

Sara frowned at her. "You told me that was next month."

"Miss O'Neill, is it? I'm Garrett, and this is Jason. We'll be conducting the inspection." One of the men stepped forward and extended his hand. Sara ignored it and after a moment he dropped it again, wiping the palm on his pants leg. "Yes, well, I can understand this is a difficult time but let me assure you, we're here for your safety."

"Felt safe until you arrived," Sara said.

Garrett shrugged. "Well, given recent events, it was thought best that we move the inspection forward."

Sara scowled. "How does someone else's incompetence…?" she began, then trailed off when she caught Nate give a little shake of his head. "Fine. Whatever."

"I was just telling these gentlemen about the generator I'm installing for you today," Nate said. His eyes kept hers as he spoke. "So you can really get started on the renovations."

"Oh." Her mouth moved like one of the dumb goldfish staring out of the tank at the play centre where she'd worked. He was giving her a safety line, she realised. A way to make it look as though she'd done more than she had. "Yes, of course. You're…earlier than I was expecting. Thanks."

He smiled that adorable asymmetrical smile she remembered from the other day. "No problem. I'll get set up while you let the inspectors know your plans for the place."

Sara swallowed. Plans? "Right. Thank you."

Garrett seemed interested. "You have plans?"

Sara led the way to the house. "Well, nothing drawn up as yet, but I've only been here a few days. I'd like to do a full restoration on the place and get it back to its original glory. They built them solid back in the day, right?"

Garrett grunted. "Not always."

Sara gritted her teeth. Diplomacy, she reminded herself. Try diplomacy. "Well, the cladding and some of the floor boards could do with replacing but the structure itself is pretty sound."

Moana gripped the porch railing and pulled hard. A chunk of wood came off in her hands.

"If you're going to deliberately damage my home, I'd rather you wait in the car," Sara snapped. "Actually, what are you even doing here?"

"I thought I should come and point out the issues," Moana said. She dropped the chunk of railing on the floor and nudged it against the wall with her foot. "This house hasn't been safe for a long time."

"Let's leave that for the inspectors to decide, shall we?" Sara tugged her dressing gown tighter around herself.

"I see you've got a pet already."

"What?" Sara looked where Moana pointed. A large ginger cat was sunning itself on the porch. She sneezed. "A stray. Gentlemen, if you'd like to start looking around, I'll go and get dressed."

She hurried down the hall to her room, kicking herself for not having spent more time cleaning up the place already. The worst of the dust and grime was gone from most of the main living areas but she was painfully aware of the parts of the house with rotted timber and moth-eaten fabrics. This was not how she would want her family's ancestral home to be assessed.

She pushed the door to her bedroom most of the way closed and dropped the dressing gown in a pool of cloth on the floor. She grabbed her jeans from beside the bed and started tugging them on.

"Just…keep in mind that the house hasn't been lived in for years and I've only just moved in, okay?" There was no response and Sara had no idea whether they'd even heard her. Probably Moana was already guiding them to the worst parts of the house. God knew how often that woman had been in here looking for the wayward offspring she'd claimed would be injured here or just sticking her nose where it didn't belong.

She pulled a bra out from under her Kindle – another flat battery, like every other electronic item in the house – and slipped it on. Next, a green t-shirt that matched her eyes. She was pulling it over her head when a creaky floorboard in the hall sounded the alarm. She jerked it down quickly, but as the cloth cleared her eyes, she saw Nate Adams standing in the doorway.

His face flushed red. "Um, sorry. I was just wondering if you had anything you wanted me to plug in…you know, to the generator once I get it started."

Sara straightened the t-shirt over her stomach. She lifted her chin, determined not to show she was embarrassed. Her insides felt hot. "Sure. My phone and charger are on the hall table."

He nodded and turned to leave.

"Nate?"

"Yes?"

"Thanks. For bringing the generator and…" She

gestured in the general direction of the rest of the house where the inspectors were doing their work.

He shrugged. "No problem."

She found the inspectors with Moana in the kitchen. Jason had an electronic stud finder pressed against the wall but seemed more interested in scratching beneath a loose flap of peeling wallpaper. Moana stood in the centre of the floor with her arms folded and a look of distaste on her face. She shivered as if someone had slipped ice down the back of her sleeveless blouse, despite the morning already being quite warm. Garrett poked behind the old wood burning stove. Sara didn't like to think what he could be finding back there.

At last he stepped back, shaking his head. "So there's no electrical wiring in the house at all?"

"Nope," Sara said. "So it will all be done fresh and up to current standards. No worries there."

The inspector frowned. "But I thought someone was electrocuted here."

"Outside. And not because of my wiring. I don't have any yet. He was supposed to be installing it. So you can't blame the house for that one." She looked pointedly at Moana.

"That doesn't mean the house is safe," Moana said. "I mean look at the rot in this door frame." She took a step forward and tripped, lurching forward like she'd been launched from a catapult. Her arms windmilled and for a moment Sara thought she would save herself, but then she stumbled further forward and her head cracked into the side of a cupboard with a loud, sickening bang. She clutched at her head and slid into a crouched position on the floor, her face a mask of pain.

"Oh God! Are you all right?"

Sara knelt beside the woman, checking her for injury.

Moana shook her off. A tiny trickle of blood ran from a cut just above her eyebrow. "I'm fine. It's your stupid uneven floor you should be worried about."

Sara bit her tongue. She stood up, wet a tea towel under the tap, and handed it to the woman to clean up the blood.

"The floor isn't uneven," Garrett said. "You tripped over this." He held up a piece of wood with paint flaking off three sides. It was the chunk of broken porch railing.

"What?" Sara stared at it. "Why did you bring that inside?"

"I didn't," Moana snapped. She pressed the wet cloth to her head and stood up slowly. "I'm not staying here. I'll wait outside."

Sara watched her leave, concerned, but satisfied that there didn't seem to be any serious damage. What she couldn't figure out was how the broken railing had ended up on the kitchen floor. It made no sense. Surely Moana wouldn't have placed it there herself and then deliberately tripped on it to make a point? She shook her head. She had bigger concerns.

"So what do you think so far?"

It was Jason who answered. "There's a lot to be done, but so far most of it is cosmetic. I don't like the look of this mould behind the wallpaper and there's a fair amount of rot. The question is whether it's gotten into any of the supporting beams. If so, that's where the problems will be. We'll let you know when we're finished."

Sara knew a dismissal when she heard one.

The low hum of the generator outside reached her as she left the building inspectors to their job. It seemed Nate had it set up and running already. That made one thing that had gone well out of this entire day. Between bad dreams, injuries, and inspections, she felt ready to go back to bed, pull the covers over her head, and hope for a better start tomorrow – and the day had barely begun!

Her shoulders slumped and she walked into the lounge and looked around, hardly daring to see the disrepair. At least the furniture here wasn't too bad. She'd folded up the sheets that had been draped over everything when she arrived and piled them up on one armchair. She sat on top of that pile, raising herself about two feet above the cushion of the actual chair, with a rueful chuckle at her need to be higher up than usual.

She closed her eyes and took a deep breath. She knew this feeling. This painful sense of being overwhelmed. It happened on every house renovation. There was always a point at which the task ahead seemed too big, too insurmountable. And there was always a point at which some part of the building code or council regulation tripped her up and meant something had to be tweaked in her plans. "That's okay," she reminded herself. "We always get through it in the end." This time she didn't have Greg's temper to deal with when things went wrong. This time, she would have to do it all on her own.

Another deep breath as she tried to centre herself the way the counsellor at the hospital had taught her. Let go of the worry. Trust in her instincts. No matter what Garrett and Jason found wrong with the house, she knew she could handle it. She would be fine.

Slowly she let her awareness focus on the sounds of the world around her. The movements of the building inspectors down the hall, the birds singing outside, the hum of the generator…the tune of a cell-phone ringing.

Her eyes popped open. She recognised that ringtone.

"Crap!"

She jumped down off the pile of linen, almost twisting her ankle as she did so. She swore again and ran for the door.

Too late.

As she stepped into the hall she saw Nate with her phone to his hear. "Sara's phone. One moment please." He held it out to her. "It started ringing almost as soon as it got any charge. I didn't want you to miss your call."

She forced a smile. "Thanks." She licked her lips and lifted the phone to her ear.

"Who the fuck was that?" Greg's voice reverberated through her like the vibration of a passing train. "Where are you?"

Sara swallowed. Her chest felt as though a thousand volts were running through her body. Her lips felt numb. "You…you're not supposed to phone me."

"Oh yeah?" The sneer was audible in his voice. "Why's that?"

"The protection order." They'd served it on him just a few hours after she'd left. That had been the plan.

"You think that shitty piece of paper is gonna stop

me finding you? You took my money, bitch. I'm coming to get it back."

Sara felt panic fluttering in her lungs like a trapped bird. "I…no…I only took my share…the lawyer said…"

"Fuck you and fuck the lawyer! Who do you think you are? You really think you can just run off in the middle of the night and I'm gonna be fine with that? You better tell me where you are right now or so help me, I'll…"

The phone pulled away from her ear and Sara let it go. She heard the soft beep as Nate hung up on the call and switched off the phone. A moment later he pulled her into a warm hug.

She stiffened against the comfort, but his strong arms around her seemed to shut away the rest of the world. Her jaw was trembling against his chest and she didn't dare look up and let him see her face, or say a word for fear of what he would see released in her – the weakness, the terror, the foolishness. What would he think of her for staying so long with a man who hit her? How could anyone respect her again?

"I'm sorry," he murmured into her hair. "I shouldn't have answered it. I didn't know."

She started to shake her head, then stopped, worried she'd smear tears onto his shirt. "It's okay. I'm okay."

"It's not okay," he said. "What he's done will never be okay. But you are. You were amazing."

The praise sent a flush of heat through her face. She didn't feel amazing. She felt like shit. And she needed to pull herself together and stop making a fool of herself in front of this man. Only a few days as his neighbour and she was already crying on his shoulder. It was ridiculous.

She pulled away and he let her go without resistance. "Thanks," she said, awkwardly. "Sorry about that."

He looked like he was going to say something in reply and she hoped it wasn't too kind because she didn't think she could take it - but then his gaze shifted and Sara heard footsteps behind her. She turned to see Garrett and Jason step into the hall. Garrett had a clipboard with several sheets of paper attached. .

"How did it go, gentlemen?" Sara asked.

Garrett unclipped the papers and held them out to her. "Unfortunately there's quite a lot of work that needs to be done to save the house, Miss O'Neill."

"Oh," she said, and took the report.

"Some of the rooms in the back of the house are currently unliveable. I've red stickered them to stay clear of because there are support beams that are too corroded in the roof."

Sara looked at the papers, then back at the building inspector. "But you're not condemning the house?"

He shook his head. "Not yet. I'd rather you stayed somewhere else, but if you stay clear of the unsafe areas, you'll be okay. You have 90 days to comply with some of the urgent issues. We will be back to check on your progress in a few weeks. I expect to see some significant changes in that time or we will have to consider alternative options."

She nodded, wondering which of them would give Moana the good news. "No problem."

"I assume you have engaged a contractor?"

"Um…" Shit. She'd intended on doing most of the work herself, but there would definitely be things she needed professionals for.

"I'll be helping out," said Nate. "I'm a registered builder as well as a sparky."

Sara blinked and stayed silent.

Garrett nodded. "Okay then. We'll be on our way and let you get to it. If you have any questions, give me a call."

He and his colleague left then, and Sara was alone with Nate once more.

"You didn't have to do that," she told him.

He shrugged. "I know. How about we make a trade? It's school holidays and I could use a babysitter for my daughter. You look after her and I'll do the wiring and heavy duty stuff around here?"

Sara blinked. She'd made a fool of herself over and over in front of this man and he still wanted to help her. She didn't know quite what to make of it. "Um."

Nate grinned. "Okay then. Come and I'll show you how to work the generator. You'll definitely want a way to charge an iPad when Abi arrives!"

CHAPTER NINE

The preliminary report in Sara's hand was many pages thick and the thought of reading through it now did nothing to dampen the headache that was threatening in the back of her sinuses. She hated crying and, worse than that, she hated being on the brink of crying and ending up red faced and runny nosed and blocked up with emotion.

At least she hadn't completely broken down in her neighbour's arms. His very strong arms and broad chest with its woodsy, masculine scent. She felt very strange about the whole Nate Adams situation, to be honest. The decisive way he had taken the phone and pulled her into an embrace had been exactly what she'd needed in her moment of weakness and pain, but she worried it was a sign of a controlling nature. Was this the kind of red flag she should have seen in Greg, and didn't?

Still, there was no denying that he'd saved her bacon today. His quick thinking to bring down the generator and make her look further along than she actually was, and his offer to assist with the wiring and rebuild of structural damage was, she was certain, a big part of the reason the inspectors had been so lenient. They could easily have forcibly evicted her from her house and she had nowhere else to go.

Time would tell whether Nate was simply a kind neighbour, another of her mistakes, or if the spark she thought she'd felt around him could be something real. For now, attractive men needed to be the last thing on her mind.

She dropped the sheaf of paper on the dining room table. She could deal with the realities brought by the building assessment later. First, she'd promised herself she would reconnect with her art. The question was, how?

She looked around for something to draw and finally settled on the photograph of great aunt Bridget and her cat. She set the frame down on the table, propped up a little by the building report, and began sketching.

Her pencil quickly blocked out the shapes of the woman's face and body, then she went back to correct the proportions she'd gotten wrong. The shoulders were a little too broad, the forehead a little too short. "Too damn out of practice," she muttered to herself.

It was strange drawing from an old black and white photograph. She wondered what the woman in the picture was really like in person. What colour had her hair been? Her eyes? Did she always seem so formal and stern or had she painted this expression on as part of the pose for the camera? The cat with her seemed an odd, softening touch.

"What were you really like?" Sara's pencil paused on her sketch as she fancied the eyes in the picture looking back at her. Two women, generations apart, living in the same house, studying each other. This was the woman the haunting rumours were about. She had to have been a character to inspire such talk.

Sara looked at her sketch. Sadly, it failed utterly to capture the unique character in Bridget's face.

She sighed. Whatever talent she'd once had was very rusty now. Still, there was a certain enjoyment in being able to see the problems, even if she couldn't yet fix them. The tension in the jaw was wrong, the cheekbones not quite high enough and the hair…she'd fallen back into the beginner's habit of making the crown of the head too small. She flipped the page over and began again on the back.

Thu-thump.

Sara sketched a few lines before the sound registered on her awareness.

Thu-thump.

She put down the pencil. It was difficult to say where it had come from but she assumed someone was knocking at the door. When she opened it, however, the porch was empty.

Thu-thump. This time it was definitely coming from inside the house.

Sara followed the sound, her breath shallow. "Hello? Anyone there?"

There was no response but the strange thumping noise, over and over, like a slow, giant heart-beat.

Her steps slow and careful, Sara made as little sound as she could moving along the corridors of the house. She peeked into a couple of rooms, trying to find the source of the noise, but always it was further along, further away.

Not for the first time, she wished she had a reliable torch or something as simple as electric lights in this house. Nate had installed a couple of lamps wired up to the generator in the front rooms, but they were too far back to be any comfort as she explored deeper towards the back of the building. Shadows crept in around her, suffocating and cold.

All the ghost stories she'd ever heard or read about seemed somehow more vivid and real now that she was alone in this abandoned house. The thumping was too regular to be an animal or a loose shutter in the wind. She didn't think Nate would be the type to play a trick on her. "Moana?" she called out. "I better not find you in my house right now. This is harassment."

Thu-thump.

She passed the stairs. The threadbare strip of carpet on the floor was frayed at the edges, the loose threads poking out like sunbeams from a child's drawing. Wallpaper pieces were peeling away from the walls.

A worse thought occurred to her. "Greg?"

Still no answer.

Thu-thump. This time she was sure it came from behind a cracked wooden door with a red sticker on it.

Sara pushed it open. The hinges creaked in protest. "Bridget?" she said, feeling silly.

The room beyond smelled damp and musty. It was dark, curtains drawn and, from the pattern of light against the fabric, the window was overgrown by ivy and wisteria on the outside. It felt cold inside and as if no other human had been in this room for a very long time. The only piece of furniture was an antique chest of drawers. The top one was open, sagging on an angle like a panting dog's tongue. As she watched, the open drawer moved on its own, wiggling up and down – thu-thump.

"What the…?"

The drawer burst into a frenzy of movement, up and down, up and down, each shift sliding it further and further from its casing. Thu-thump, thu-thump, thu-thump, thu-thump. Then – BANG – it slipped entirely off the track and hit the floor, splitting apart into little more than kindling.

Among the pieces was an old leather-bound journal, grey with dust.

Sara's heart was thumping as swiftly as the drawer had done. Her chest felt tight and her skin cold. It was an animal, she told herself. Some large rat or kea was hiding behind the drawer, pushing it out.

But there was nothing in the gap.

A gust of wind blew open the journal, scattering the dust clumps like drab glitter across the floor. The page had large letters hand written in flowing script: The Private Diary of Miss Bridget O'Neill.

Sara swallowed. This was impossible. It couldn't be real. Could it?

She gritted her teeth, then swooped down to snatch up the book before running from the room and slamming the door behind her. The house was darker and colder as she hurried back to the dining room. Even Nate Adams's lamps seemed hard pressed to push away the shadows.

It was a good ten minutes of silence in the house and a warm cup of tea chasing away her fears before Sara, at last, opened the diary at random and began to read.

CHAPTER TEN

13 August, 1835

We've completely finished the cellar now and started on the main level of the house. Thank the Lord we're done with all that digging and lugging stone. If Jereth hadn't been here to help us with it we'd have hardly scratched the surface. His people's ways are surprising and exciting to watch.

Papa and Nan say the upper levels will go much more quickly and certainly there's no lack of timber in these parts. It's just a matter of utilising what is close at hand. Papa has built many a fine house back home and he insists ours will be the best of any of them.

He doesn't like the other settlers coming up to our land though and I believe I now see why. Yesterday, I visited Tammy Connor at her family's land down by the bay, and she says they all pitch in to help each other and it takes whole teams of oxen to shift the native kauri tree logs. They would be shocked to see how quickly we can do it with Jereth's help. Nan says we should always be careful not to stick out too much in folk's minds in case they blame us for the bad things that come. I think she's worried they'd want too much of our help and there'd be no time for making Papa's vision for our new home come true.

Jereth is eager for Nan and I to finish our own work in the forest. Last night, he told me he will speak with his parents as soon as we are done and tell them how we feel about each other. Intermarrying is unusual but not unheard of. He simply needs permission to go ahead with our plans.

For myself, I am more concerned with the reactions of my own family. I believe that, for all our people have a history of consorting with his, the thought of Jereth and I being together will be something beyond their understanding.

So for now we must try our best to remain proper when we are together but it is so difficult to stay my hand when it desires so ardently to reach out for his touch. When he is not near me, I think of him and I long to wear his ring but I cannot. No one can know of our love until the time is right. So I watch him from a distance, all strength and shining beauty, and long for a time when he will truly be mine.

It could take a while though. We were visited by the local Maori again today. This time they brought their Kuia. I think she's a wise woman, much like Nan. She spoke to us about our work in the forest and told us they believe what we are doing is dangerous. She called Nan and I kauwaka, and said we were fooling with things that are sacred and should not be touched.

I thought we had left the fear and ignorance behind

in Ireland but this new country seems almost as bad. Maori have their own magic, Nan says. It may be that we will need them and their guardianship of this land to complete our task. For Jereth's sake and my own happiness, I hope we can convince them of the purity of our mission.

CHAPTER ELEVEN

A loud banging on the front door jerked Sara from sleep. She flipped Bridget's journal closed and rubbed at her face where she'd been resting on the hard wooden table. Dozing off during the day was very unlike her but it seemed she'd been more worn out by the stress of the morning than she'd thought.

The front door creaked loudly. Sara got to her feet. "Who's there?"

"Hello? Sara? Are you home?" It was the little girl she'd met the other day.

Of course. Sara sighed in relief. She'd promised Nate she would babysit when he was working. "In here, Abigail."

The girl was wearing grey trousers and a small pink bomber jacket with her hair in pigtails. "Dad said I should come over here for the afternoon instead of going to Auntie Moana's."

Sara nodded. "That's fine. When does your dad finish work today?"

"I dunno..." The little girl shrugged and her gaze

slid over the table to Sara's earlier sketches. "Did you draw those?"

"Yeah, I did."

"Wow."

Sara smiled. Kids were so easy to impress sometimes. "Tell you what, how about you help me strip some wallpaper and then we can do some drawing together later?"

Abi stared at her. "Strip wallpaper?"

"Yeah. I'm renovating. Watch." She found where the building inspectors had poked at the wall, grabbed a lifting edge and pulled. A long strip of paper peeled away like a banana skin.

Abigail's eyes widened.

"You want a turn?"

The little girl reached up and worked her fingertips into a crease, then paused and looked at Sara for confirmation.

"Go on," Sara said. "But only ever do this on the walls I tell you to, okay? We're doing it so we can put up new paper." And probably new jib board for that matter, but explaining construction to a seven year old seemed unnecessary just yet.

Abigail tugged and the paper came away with a satisfying ripping sound. She giggled and clapped her hands. "Can I do it again?"

Sara laughed with her. "You bet. Let's do this whole wall. You take the bottom half and I'll do the top."

The afternoon went by quickly after that. Both Abigail and Sara were having fun with their planned destruction, tearing strips of paper from the wall. Much of it came away easily, the glue long since degraded. For the rest, they used rags with warm water to soak and then peel away with fingernails or a butter knife.

This was part of the process Sara had always enjoyed. It felt like the house were some growing insect and she was helping it to moult out of its old skin, into the beautiful creature it would become. The colours and clean, new vibrancy were not there yet, but the potential was, lurking beneath the tired, dirty, mouldy exterior of each wall. It was a new beginning. And those were always full of promise.

As she stripped away the old paper of the house, Sara could feel her old life and fears falling away as well. "Race you," she said to Abigail, and the two of them began tearing at the wall even faster. Strips of paper fell like confetti across the floor and the sound of their laughter filled the room.

Finally, they reached the end and stepped back, huge grins on both their faces.

"Good job," Sara said, picking a loose piece of wallpaper from Abi's hair.

"That was fun!" Abi said, wrapping her little arms around Sara's legs in a hug. "You're fun. Auntie Moana would never let me do something like that."

Sara could well imagine she wouldn't. Moana seemed like she'd be the authoritarian type. "Well, your Auntie probably hasn't been redecorating her house recently," she said. "And you must only peel off wallpaper if the owner of the house says it's okay."

Abi nodded and pulled back. Her eyes wide. "So you own this house now?"

Sara let her hand teeter side to side. "Sort of. My

family does. I'm the one living here at the moment."

"I hope you stay."

Sara smiled. "Thanks, Abi. Now how about we clean up this mess and then have a drink and do some drawing?"

They settled down at the table with a piece of paper each. Abigail had a set of coloured pencils that she'd brought with her and happily used them to draw colourful pictures of fairies and ponies.

Sara watched the girl work and let her own pencil sketch out her features. This time her skills worked better. She'd always been better drawing from life than from a photograph. After half an hour, despite the girl's inability to sit still, she had a fairly decent likeness of Abi's studious expression, chubby cheeks and intense eyes as she worked with her coloured pencils.

Sara used her finger to smudge a final bit of shading and sat back to study her work. Not bad.

Abigail also sat back, seemingly happy with what she'd done.

"So what have you drawn, Abi?"

The little girl turned the page sideways so Sara could get a better look and pointed to some of the colourful figures. "That's you and this is your castle."

The castle looked suspiciously like a squashed box with cotton wool trees beside it, but Sara nodded and made encouraging sounds.

"And this is the fairy prince come to marry you. He's going to live in the castle and you'll have a baby and live happily ever after."

Sara felt numb. The colours on Abigail's drawing seemed to pulse in time with her heartbeat. Her prince had been a monster, not a fairy. And her baby…her baby was all the proof she needed to know she didn't deserve a happily ever after.

Her fingers clenched, scrunching paper into her palm. Her own drawing. Was it Abigail she had drawn? Or some wistful dream of what her own child might have been if she'd lived? If she'd trusted her mother to take care of her.

Abi was staring at her. "Don't you like it?"

Sara forced herself to smile. "Of course I do. It's beautiful. Thank you." She stood up from the table. "How about a drink of water?"

Without waiting for an answer, she strode quickly across to the kitchen. Her jaw tight, she swallowed hard, forcing the emotion down.

She held out her hand and let go of her drawing. The sketch of a child slipped softly into the rubbish bin.

CHAPTER TWELVE

Nate felt a dull throbbing pain building at the base of his skull as he pulled on the handbrake and got out of the car at the old O'Neill place. The sun was low and he squinted against the glare as he looked over the house. There was a lot of work to be done – that much had always been obvious at a glance – but Sara was right: the majority of the building was structurally sound and it was worth saving. He just wondered how much she would be counting on him to save it.

Moana had been in his ear for the last hour as he'd finished up the accounts for the day's jobs back at the shop. He should have known she would be after he'd come to Sara's rescue this morning. If he'd had any sense at all he would have taken the paper work home or simply left it for tomorrow, but he hated leaving the business untidy if he could avoid it and he knew from experience that there would be little time or energy for it after an evening with his seven year old daughter.

Other dads might be able to take time out while their wives entertained the kids, but Nate didn't have that luxury. People always said solo parenting was tough but he'd never fully appreciated how much easier life had been with Emma until she was gone. She always seemed to understand their daughter so much better than he did. God knew what he would do when it came time to talk about bras and tampons. Still, the least he could do was give her his attention when he was home with her. He might not be able to give the girl her mother back, but he was determined to give her as much of a father as he could.

Too much, if Moana was to be believed. His doting was one of her usual favourite topics. Not today, however.

"What were you thinking?" Moana had called out, almost before he'd made it through the door of the shop. "Are you that easily taken in by a pretty face?"

Nate, his head still full of details for the day's jobs had looked completely blank.

"The girl next door with the falling down house that she's convinced you to help her patch up? Those must be some mighty fine eyelashes she's been batting at you, boy. Or is it something lower down? I get that it's been a while for you, but…"

"Hey," Nate's voice was nearly a growl. "A little more respect please. For your sister's memory if not for me. And Sara has done nothing wrong, so why don't you leave her to sort out her house in peace for a bit?"

"Her being here is wrong," Moana muttered. "She's stirring up things that should be left alone."

As he climbed the steps to the porch, Nate had to

admit Sara had stirred up something. He found her intriguing. He had since their coffee and conversation the other day at his house. At the time, he'd wondered what he'd done to send her running off so quickly. After this morning, he began to understand. The phone call from a man who was obviously her ex – an ex she was very clearly afraid of – explained a lot.

Nate's own sister had dealt with an abusive partner for three years before finally finding the courage to leave him and Nate, only nineteen at the time, had hated the necessity of walking the tightrope whenever he'd been around them. He couldn't stand by and pretend nothing was happening – he had to stand up for his sister. But he had to be careful not to make things worse until she was ready. And when she had finally been ready he'd been the one she came to. He'd driven her to the airport and she'd started a new life in Brisbane.

Nate knew how hard it had to have been for Sara to leave her life behind. If he wanted her to be anything more than neighbourly, he was going to have to prove that a man could be trusted after all.

He shooed away a couple of stray cats, sunning themselves on the porch, knowing they would likely mess with Sara's allergies if she saw them. The creatures really did seem to be attracted to her. He could well relate.

As he knocked on the door, he wondered briefly if he'd done the right thing asking Sara to babysit. Abigail and Moana seemed to clash more often than not so it'd seemed logical to jump at the chance for a qualified early childhood educator to keep her busy over the holidays.

A large plastic rubbish bag sat in the corner of the porch, the top open to reveal hundreds of scraps of paper. Nate peered in while he waited. Sure enough, the bag was full of torn up wallpaper. He chuckled. So much for his worries that Sara might be the sort of woman who would take advantage of his offer of help. She'd already gotten on with the renovations without him. And she'd been babysitting Abigail all afternoon.

He was turning back to the door when something among the scraps caught his eye. It was a page from a notebook, tucked amongst the wallpaper. On it, was a perfect likeness of Abigail.

Nate picked it up. It really was her. Sketched in pencil, every line in place, every curve. He smiled. There was a definite twinkle in her eye that was Abigail. And the slope of her nose that was just as Emma's had been. And the rogue curl in her hair that he could never brush straight. It was perfect.

Had Sara done this? And then thrown it out? Did she really underestimate her talent that much?

The door opened and he spun around, quickly tucking the sketch behind his back. The last thing he wanted Sara to think was that he'd been going through her rubbish like some homeless stalker.

"Daddy!" Abigail flew across the porch like a pigtailed tui diving to its nest.

Nate managed to stuff the sketch into his back pocket just in time to catch his laughing daughter as she flung herself into his arms. Her pink bomber jacket was half on and half off, making her lopsidedly puffy, like a half melted marshmallow. "Did you have fun?"

She nodded, her pigtails flapping like little wings.

"So much fun. Sara's cool, Dad. She let me help her do wallpaper."

Nate looked over at Sara, who stood in the doorway. "Thank you. I should have a couple of hours early afternoon tomorrow if you want me to get started on the wiring."

"That'd be great." Sara held out Abi's schoolbag. "She was a pleasure to have over and a big help. It was nice to have some company. This huge house gets a bit lonely by myself sometimes."

Nate nodded. "Well, how about you come over for dinner this weekend? I'm not bad company either."

"Oh, I didn't mean…" Sara's cheeks flushed a charming pink.

He chuckled. "I know. But I'd like to have you over. It's the neighbourly thing to do, after all."

"Well…"

"We can talk about your plans for the house. Come on. Let me cook for you."

Abigail was bouncing on the balls of her feet. "Pleeeeeease."

Sara caved. "Okay. If I can return the favour sometime."

Nate smiled. "Deal."

And the smile stayed on his face all the way home.

CHAPTER THIRTEEN

"You're going to need a lot of new cladding," Nate said, rapping on the wall in one of the bedrooms. "Some of this is definitely rotted."

Sara sighed. "I know. And we'll have to replace some of the internal beams as well. It's held up pretty well though, for such an old house. The inspectors' report could have been a lot worse." She bit down on the words she wanted to say: if Moana had gotten her way, the house would have been condemned on the spot and they'd be assessing a pile of rubble by now. Much as she disliked the woman, Sara didn't like to speak badly about Abigail's aunt in front of the girl.

"I could give you a ride into town if you like. Take you to get supplies." He nodded his head in the direction of his ute, parked outside. "They charge a lot for delivery out here and you'll get the tradie discount if I'm with you."

Sara chewed her lip, thinking. "When you say 'town' you mean…?"

"Whangarei's the closest big city." He gave a wry chuckle. "You thinking Auckland?"

She swallowed. "Yeah, but Whangarei's fine. I'm sure you know the good places." The last thing she wanted to do was go back to Auckland and risk going to the building supply shops she'd gone to with Greg. "It's still a long way though. Are you sure you want to drive that far?"

"Depends on the company." He grinned. "But I need to order a few things myself anyway so it's no hassle."

The inside of Nate's ute was a curious mix of electrical wire spools, a toolbox, an old pair of overalls, and three Barbie dolls. Abigail ensconced herself in the centre of the cab and immediately picked up one of the dolls in a sparkling evening gown and gossamer wings. She began brushing the doll's hair as if it were the most important thing in the world and seemed oblivious to the seatbelt being clicked into place around her by her father before he gunned the engine into life and guided them out onto the main road.

"Big city, here we come." Nate flicked on the radio and shot Sara a smile. "Well, medium city, anyway."

She smiled back, but it felt forced. Her eyes were drawn back to Abigail's doll. Was that the kind of thing her daughter would have liked to play with if she'd been born? If she'd trusted Sara enough to let herself come into this world.

Sara turned to stare out the window. The tiny town of Kowhiowhio passed by in a damp blur. She wiped her eyes and swallowed as the last building gave way to bush and farmland. "Suck it up, girl," she told herself, imagining her grandmother's voice. It was just as well she wasn't still working at her old kindergarten if the sight of a doll could get her this emotional.

She took a deep breath and watched the landscape passing by as they made their way around the winding road. Nate was careful to slow the car down a little before each corner.

Gradually Sara noticed music from the radio. It was a high energy pop station. Not quite what she'd imagined Nate would be listening to. Beside her, Abigail sang loudly along with each song. Amusingly, Nate sang with her – with reasonable tunefulness – but only the last half of each line of lyrics.

"What are you grinning at?" Nate asked, glancing across the cab at her.

"Nothing." Sara smiled back. This time it was for real. "You're a good driver," she said. "I like that. Makes me feel safe."

Nate was silent for a long moment, watching the road. He gripped the steering wheel very tight with one hand and briefly rubbed at his face with the other before bringing it back to the wheel. "Good," he said, softly. "Better safe than sorry, right?"

"Right." Sara watched him, wondering what she'd said wrong.

He didn't look at her or speak for a several minutes. Nor did he start singing again.

It was Abigail who spoke up, tapping Sara on the arm. "Do you want a turn with my fairy doll? I'm going to play with the other one now."

Sara took the offered doll with a smile. "Thank you, Abi. That's very kind of you. She's very pretty."

The little girl nodded. "Fairy princesses always are."

Sara chuckled. "I suppose so."

The rest of the trip passed in animated chatter about dolls and kittens, with Nate proving to know a surprising amount about both. Each of the Barbies had a back-story and clearly Abigail's doting dad had been indoctrinated in all of them.

When they pulled the ute into the carpark at the building supply store in Whangarei, Sara had forgotten her melancholy of earlier and had found she too was singing along to the radio. The three of them created a sound quite unlike anything the musicians had intended but full of joy and laughter nonetheless.

"So do you have an idea of what you want to get while we're here?" Nate asked, as the automatic doors swooshed open.

"Jib board, some beams – you've got tools to cut things down to size, I'm assuming?"

He nodded.

"Good. Then some paint – I've got some ideas for the colours I'm after but I'll have to look at the range they have here. Some of the curtains will need replacing too, so we should see if they have fabric swatches I can look through. If you see anything that seems like it'd go with that vine motif, let me know. I want to keep as much of that as I can. It's so integral to the character of the house. And I should get some sandpaper and varnish and…" She trailed off. Nate was staring at her, grinning. "What?"

"I think this is the most animated I've seen you since you got here. You really like this stuff, don't you?"

Sara felt her stomach tighten a little and tried to keep her tone from getting defensive. "Yeah, I do. And I'm good at it."

Nate nodded. "I don't doubt it. Let's get to work."

Sara blinked. She'd been expecting an argument. Greg would never have let her take charge like that without trying to cut her down to size. Shopping with Nate was very different. He listened to her ideas and made suggestions but left it to her to decide. Each time she picked something from a shelf, she had her arguments and justifications ready. Each time, they went unsaid.

"Nice," Nate commented as she added a leaf stencil to the cart along with some paints. "Continuing the vine thing."

"Motif," said Sara. "Yeah." Her emotions churned inside her, as jumbled as the pigments being combined in the paint mixer. Should she smile and trust his support or frown and be wary of it? Nate had been nothing but helpful and supportive since her arrival in town. Was she being unfair to judge him by the expectations she'd developed for Greg?

They continued strolling the aisles, with Abigail perched on the front of the cart like the figurehead of an old fashioned ship. She clung to the metal cart and squealed with delight.

Sara chuckled. "I'm king of the world," she quoted.

Nate laughed. It was nice to hear a man laugh with her and in appreciation of her. It'd been a long time since she'd had that. It gave her a warm tingle in her chest. She liked it.

"Do they stock light fittings?" Sara forced herself

back to the job at hand. "If you're going to wire up the place, we're going to need them."

"They do." He nodded and led the way with the cart.

The collection of light fittings was a small one and mainly simple, modern styles. Frosted globes, shaded lamps, and rows and rows of swirl-shaped eco-bulbs. At one end of the aisle was a large, elaborate chandelier, dripping with crystals. It was a beauty and spat little shards of light across the floor like a scattering of diamonds. She stared at it, trying to picture where in the house it might fit. The hall would be too small and it was too ostentatious for the living room. Perhaps over the staircase?

She sighed. "Too expensive anyway, I'm sure."

As she turned away, her eyes caught something on a lower shelf – a kind of mini chandelier with arms in the shape of vines with flowers at the end to hold the bulbs. Vines again. Perfect.

She reached out for it and Nate did the same. Their fingers touched as they both grabbed it together. The metal of the vines was cool to the touch but Nate's skin was warm. Sara jerked her hand back, her face red. "Sorry."

Nate smiled and pulled the light fitting from the shelf. "Great minds think alike. I knew you'd be keen as soon as I saw it." He lifted it into the cart.

Sara couldn't help but clap her hands in delight, grinning as Abigail did the same. "Let's see if they can order in some more in the same style. It'd be great to have them throughout the house."

"I bet the other lady would like that one too," said

Abigail as they strolled toward the counter.

Sara frowned. "What other lady?" The only other woman she knew in Kowhiowhio was Moana and somehow she didn't think a decorative light fixture would change that woman's opinion of her home.

The little girl shrugged. "The one that lived in your house."

"You mean my grandmother? She hasn't lived there in years. No one has."

Abigail tugged at the hem of her jacket and stayed silent.

"Abi had an imaginary friend for a while," Nate supplied. "She apparently lived in your house."

"Oh." Sara stopped walking.

Nate, Abi and the cart carried on a few steps without her before Nate noticed and turned back. "You okay?"

"Yeah, fine." She swallowed her sense of dread. Yet another strange occurrence connected to the house. Even as she told herself all children have imaginary friends, she had to ask – how many times could she call it a coincidence?

CHAPTER FOURTEEN

"I don't think it's a date." Sara paced the living room with the phone pressed to her ear. A collection of sledge hammers, screwdrivers, levels and other tools was piled in the corner like some construction worker version of a game of pick-up-sticks. A single lamp powered by the generator outside kept the room lit despite a gloomy, cloud covered sky outside. Several of the walls had newly installed power sockets, the plastic shiny and out of place in the old décor. Wires hung from the ceiling ready for a light fitting to be installed when it arrived. She was having them sent up from Whangarei.

"It's a date." Her grandmother's voice was adamant.

"But we've just been working together. I look after his daughter and he's helping me with the house. I think it's a friendly neighbour thing."

"Any time a man cooks for you, my dear, it's a date. He sounds nice. Enjoy it. You deserve to have a nice evening with a man and not worry about him hitting you." Sara wondered if there was a touch of reproach in the old woman's voice or if she was imagining it. Her grandmother, like everyone else, had wanted her to leave Greg a long time ago. The rest had gradually fallen away, unable or unwilling to be a support. Her grandmother was her only constant.

"But…you don't think it's too soon?"

A snort echoed through the phone. "At my age, Sara, there's no such thing as too soon. Life isn't about waiting, my dear. You deserve a little happiness and a little fun. If you enjoy his company, there's no need to deny yourself that."

She did enjoy his company. These few days of working on the house together had shown her that. She'd found herself looking forward to the few hours Nate could spare from his paying jobs to help her.

Unlike many of the sparkies and builders she'd dealt with back in Auckland, Nate seemed to really respect her opinions and her abilities when it came to renovating the house. He asked questions to clarify what she'd need help with and left her to do the rest without watching or critiquing the job when she was done – something Greg had never been able to stop doing. He even admired her choices and noticed when she'd thought about things like where the best place for lights and plug sockets would be to suit the shape of the room.

On top of that, he was funny and charming. He had a cute way of talking to himself while he worked and his comments were often extremely witty. She'd smothered laughter on many occasions as he scrambled through the roof laying wires. And it was clear he loved his daughter very much. Working at a kindergarten, she'd seen the dads who just phoned it in, picking up their kids on the way home from work, exhausted or doing their duty for the weekend visitation with the new girlfriend in tow. Nate wasn't like that. He paid attention to Abigail and listened to her when she talked. It was nice to see.

"How does a man treat children, animals and service staff?" Grandma always said. "That will tell you about his character." So far, Nate Adams seemed like a good guy.

So far.

"My taste in men is so shit."

"Nonsense. You made one poor choice and you stuck with it. Perseverance is usually a good thing. Have you learned from your experience?"

Sara exhaled, staring ruefully at the ceiling. "Yeah. Yeah, I have."

"Then all is not lost in that pretty little head of yours. It's okay to get back on the horse, Sara. Just be more aware this time and take care of yourself."

As she hung up the phone, Sara wondered about her grandmother's words. There might be a few things lost in her head after all. She hadn't mentioned the dizzy spells or strange dreams she'd been having to her grandmother for fear of worrying her, but they had both increased as the days went on. Last night, she'd awakened to find herself sleepwalking in the hallway. She'd been on her way to the circular pond she'd found in the bush but, once awake, had no idea why she would go there.

She told herself it was the lingering effects of the late term miscarriage and electric shock she'd received but…somehow she felt sure it was more than that. Something was happening to her in this house. Something was here with her.

"Idiot," she muttered to herself. She was letting the ghost stories get to her. That or some sort of post-traumatic stress. It was ridiculous. "What I should be worrying about is what to wear to this dinner."

If this really was a date, she wanted to make a good impression. But it'd been years since she'd even thought about dating. What did women wear for dates these days? How dressed up should she be to go to a man's house for dinner? Somehow a little black dress seemed too formal, but jeans and a t-shirt might look like she wasn't interested.

And, she admitted to herself, she was interested.

Her feelings for Greg had evaporated long ago. Now that she'd broken the ties that had bound her to him, there was nothing but relief. Nate was part of her fresh start. Why shouldn't she explore the possibility of a relationship with him? Or, at the very least, a friendship? What outfit could say all that *and* be date appropriate?

"Okay," she muttered. "Time to try on some clothes."

She headed toward the door when the lamp in the corner flickered. Sara stopped. Her chest tightened and the room seemed to tilt. She stumbled, catching herself on the back of the sofa to keep from falling.

The lightbulb buzzed like a wasp in a jar, louder and louder, as though the insect was rattling between her ears, until the sound separated out into words and voices. "Come here. Help us. Come to us."

The floor gave way and her legs plunged into cold water, the shock of it sending sparks of alarm throughout her body.

“Let us out,” the buzzing whispered. “Set us free.”

“Stop that!” She shook her head and forced the voices out. The light fell back into a steady glow, and the sound stopped.

Gasping for breath, Sara straightened up and looked around. The room was as it was. Her legs were dry. Nothing had changed.

Almost nothing.

As she turned, Sara saw a figure in the doorway. She wore a striped bodice, high necked blouse, long, deep green skirt, her hair up in a tight bun, a rifle in her left hand. Bridget stepped forward into the light. Her skin was pale, almost paper white. Her hair was the colour of whipped shadows and her eyes glowed a phosphorescent green.

“Do not trust them,” she said, her voice breathy and hoarse. “Read my words.”

Then she vanished in a shower of sparks.

CHAPTER FIFTEEN

Sara still felt shaken as she arrived at Nate and Abigail's house. Her pulse had been a living thing in her ears as she'd gotten ready for the date. There'd been no further sign of strangeness and her dizzy spell had completely gone, but, try as she might, she couldn't dismiss what she'd seen. The stories about Bridget haunting the house…well, they weren't just stories.

She took a deep breath. For all that it'd been scary, there seemed no reason to think Bridget wanted to harm her. Or perhaps her years with Greg had left her jaded to the potential for harm. She gave a cynical laugh. Compared to him, a disembodied spirit didn't seem so bad.

Bridget's warning about trust was ambiguous at best. Chances are, whomever the spirit was worried about was long dead anyway. But if she wanted Sara to read her diary - well, that was easy enough.

After her date.

"She's waited a couple hundred years already. One

more night isn't gonna kill her," Sara muttered to herself as she stepped up to the door. She straightened her back, smoothed out the sleeveless top she'd worn over a floral skirt, and knocked.

A moment later the door opened to reveal a side of Nate she hadn't seen before. He'd obviously showered and dressed up for the occasion, making her glad she'd believed her grandmother's advice about it being a date. He wore dress pants and a blue shirt that brought out the colour in his eyes. His hair was still damp and brushed in a dark sweep back from his forehead and the smell of spicy cologne mixed with a delicious aroma of roast tomatoes and cheese and something else that made her mouth water.

He smiled when he saw her, and she couldn't help but respond in kind. The warmth in his eyes soothed the tension she held tight inside her and she relaxed. Then his hand touched her shoulder as he ushered her inside, sending a jolt of searing heat through her skin.

"I'm glad you made it," he said and sounded like he meant it.

Sara flushed and glanced away, quickly passing him to enter the room. "Something smells delicious."

"Thanks," Nate said, closing the door and placing a hand on the small of her back to guide her toward the kitchen area. He lifted one of two glasses of wine that were waiting and handed it to her. "I'm making lasagne. My speciality."

"I'm impressed."

"Wait until you taste it before you commit."

She smiled into her glass. It'd been a long time since anyone had cooked for her. "I'm sure it will be lovely."

"I hope so. It's been a while since I cooked for anyone but me and Abi."

Sara looked around. "Where is Abi?"

"In bed. That's why I suggested a late dinner. I wanted us to have some adult time."

Sara raised an eyebrow. "Oh?"

He laughed, his face flushing adorably. "Not like that! I just mean it will be nice for us to be able to talk without having to worry what she's up to."

Sara laughed too. "I know what you mean. After a day looking after kids, it was always nice to converse with grownups. Abi's a great kid though. You must be very proud."

"I am." There was no trace of anything but warmth in his voice. "Very much."

Sara watched as he slipped on oven mitts, pulled the sizzling, deep dish lasagne from the oven, then served it onto plates next to a salad. He shook up a bottle of dressing and deftly drizzled just enough over the rocket leaves and cherry tomatoes.

"I thought we could eat outside," he said, handing her one of the plates. "It's a warm night. Plus, it'll be kinder on your allergies. The cat spends most of his time sleeping on the dining room chairs."

"That sounds nice," she said, and started to follow him when something on the wall stopped her in her tracks. It was the sketch she'd done of Abigail, framed and hanging in pride of place in the lounge.

She put the plate back down on the bench. "Where did you get that?"

Nate turned back to see what she was pointing at and

his face flushed red. "Oh. I saw it and it was so good that…I should have asked. I'm sorry."

Sara frowned. "I threw it out."

"Yeah. But Abigail loves it so much and so do I. You really are talented, you know." He dipped his head a little to catch her eye. "Is it okay? I didn't think you wanted it."

Sara swallowed. "Um…yeah, I guess. I just wasn't expecting it is all." She picked up her plate again and followed him out onto the veranda, trying to sort through her feelings as she did so.

She'd never expected to have her art appreciated up here. Never thought to show it to anyone. Certainly not yet. To think that Nate had found something she'd discarded as not good enough and had it framed and hung in his home gave her a shocking warm feeling inside. He liked what she'd done. He meant it. "Thank you," she said quietly. "That's quite a compliment."

Nate shrugged. "Well, it's true."

As they stepped out onto the veranda, she saw a small picnic table had been laid with cutlery and flowers and a few dozen tea-light candles were scattered around, giving the whole area a warm, flickering glow. The fragrance of freesias and daphne was still in the night air and the stars twinkled overhead like sparkling confetti.

"This is beautiful," Sara said, putting her plate down and taking a seat.

Nate helped her with her chair, then sat opposite. "It seems to be going around," he said, with a nod in her direction.

She laughed. "Cheesy."

"But true again."

They ate quietly for a while, the sound of cicadas and the occasional morepork providing background music in the darkness. The food was a symphony of rich flavours, each bite more tasty than the last.

"This is so good," Sara said at last.

"I considered being a chef at one point," Nate said. "But didn't fancy the hours. I'm too much of a family man at heart. I wouldn't want to miss evenings at home."

"Fair enough. Did you grow up in Kowhiowhio? Or was somewhere else home originally?"

"Born in Auckland but left the big smoke when I got married. Emma's Iwi were from up here and she wanted to be close to her family and land and all that. They're Abi's iwi too, so I stuck around. It's a nice town when you get used to it."

Sara washed down a bite of lasagne with a sip of wine. "I'm sure."

"How do you think you're settling in? Aside from the obvious."

"The obvious being Moana's little vendetta? Yeah, I think I'm settling in okay. It's…not what I'm used to." She thought about all the strange occurrences that had taken place at the house. "It's been strange."

"How so?"

Sara stared into the darkness beyond the candles, wondering just what to say.

"Do you believe in ghosts?" she asked quietly.

Nate hesitated, his head tilting to one side. "I believe people see and feel what they need to about the ones they've lost." He raised his glass to his lips and took a sip before setting it down with a shrug. "For a long time after Emma died, I could feel her presence with me. I had no idea what to do with the life we had made together or how to raise our daughter on my own. I needed her spirit to be there. It helped me. For a while. And then it didn't."

Sara reached out and touched his hand with hers. "What happened then?"

He put his other hand over hers. "I got over it. Eventually. It took a long time though and Moana was a huge support to us during that time. She…she took Abigail for a while. When I couldn't cope. I think maybe she still thinks of me as not coping. But…it was a long time ago now."

Sara nodded slowly. "Do you still feel Emma's presence?"

"No." Nate shook his head. "I still talk to her now and then, and think about what she would say, but no. She's gone." He looked up from their hands and gave a wry smile. "She believed though. I know that much. Her family are the spiritual leaders in the tribe. She was considered a *kuia*."

Sara's eyes widened. "She must have been very young for the title. I thought that was reserved for older, wise women."

"It is." Nate's eyes grew unfocussed as he stared into the past. "She had a lot of *mana* for someone her age. There was just something about her." He blinked and looked back at Sara. "Reminds me of you in that way. I think she would have liked you."

Sara snorted. "Not if her sister's anything to go by."

"Ha! Emma and Moana were nothing alike. Believe me, I chose the right sister."

Sara felt her smile fade. "Well, I guess you were better at choosing than I was."

Nate's eyes met hers, gentle and strong. "What happened with you and your ex?"

"I…" She tried to put on the brave face. The fake smile. The oh-it's-nothing-just-a-little-accident-I'm-totally-okay mask she'd worn for all her friends and colleagues and family for so long. She tried but it didn't fit her any more. She didn't want to hide what had happened. Not from herself. Not from Nate.

"I fell in love and he hit me," she said. The words were somehow a relief to say. She took a deep breath and continued. "He hit me a lot, actually. I always made an excuse for it. He was stressed – we both were. He was apologetic after. He loved me. I loved him. Then after a while there was no excuse any more but I still couldn't make myself leave. The excuses were for me after that. We were financially committed to whatever house project we were working on at the time and it would be too hard to leave."

She glanced up at Nate. His expression was thoughtful, sympathetic. She'd expected anger or frustration. Maybe even disgust.

"That sounds incredibly hard," he said. "How did you manage to get out?"

She bit her lip. This next part was the hardest. "My latest reason for staying was that I got pregnant. I thought maybe the idea of being a father would change him somehow." She shook her head. It sounded so stupid out loud. "It didn't. I…ended up in hospital a couple of times. Lot of bruises and then a late term miscarriage."

"Oh God." Nate reached across the table to hold her hand.

"When the baby died I realised what a fool I'd been. We'd just sold our most recent house project so I took the car and my share of the money and I ran. There's a protection order against him but he still texts and tries to phone me every day."

"You know that's not your fault, right?"

"What isn't?"

"Him hitting you. The baby. All of it."

She stared at the table. Suddenly it seemed ridiculous but she did think it was her fault. "If I'd been stronger," she started, "then my baby might have…"

Nate shook his head. "No. That's not true. I know it's easy to think that – believe me, I know. When Emma died, I kept questioning over and over what I should have done differently so that she wouldn't be on that road at that time. But the truth is, nothing I did put that truck in her path. It just was. And nothing you did caused this. It just is."

He stood up and came around the table and pulled her to her feet and into his arms. The warmth of him seemed to penetrate her chest and spread from her heart to fill every cell of her body. The smell of him filled her lungs, comforting and kind. This time there was no stopping the flow of tears as he held her. But they were soft, gentle tears. A letting go and a mourning, not the uncontrollable wailing she'd feared for so long.

Nate held her as she cried, and she clung to him like an anchor, a grounding influence in the world of abuse and ghosts and madness. The tears cleansed her. When they stopped, she felt released.

She stepped back, wiping her eyes. “Sorry. Didn’t mean to fall apart on you again.”

Nate reached up and brushed a damp strand of hair from her face. “You didn’t. You’ve been incredibly strong for a long time. It’s fine to lean on someone else for a while.”

“Thank you.” She found her hand somehow stroking his chest as if it belonged there. The muscles beneath his shirt were hard and strong.

“No problem.” His fingers traced down her arm, a tingling trail of heat. “How about I go get us some dessert?”

She smiled. “Sounds good.”

Nate disappeared inside the house and Sara waited, hugging herself and trying to analyse the date.

Her emotional outpouring notwithstanding, she felt that things were going well. Nate seemed an even nicer guy than she’d thought and had been understanding and able to put her at ease when talking about her history. Perhaps discussing their past relationships wasn’t recommended first date practice, but they’d known each other for a little while now so it made sense that they deepen their knowledge of each other tonight.

She wondered how much to tell him about what had been happening at the house. Should she mention Bridget’s ghost having made an appearance earlier today? Or would that be the thing that snuffed out the understanding in his eyes? She couldn’t help thinking she’d pushed her luck too much already.

“Stop being so serious about every damn thing, Sara,” she muttered to herself. “It’s a date. Just have fun.”

How did people have fun on dates these days? And what was it her grandmother had said? "Just get back on the horse."

Could she? It'd been a while since she'd "been on the horse" so to speak. Greg hadn't touched her in that way since she'd gotten pregnant and he'd been the only man to do so in a long time. Perhaps it was time to fully purge him from her system.

There was no denying that she found Nate attractive. The sensation of his touch was still on her skin. He was a nice guy. They both deserved a little "adult time" and she needed to feel wanted again.

She took a deep breath and popped the uppermost button on her top. Time to give it a shot.

Nate walked back out with a parfait glass in each hand, brimming with cream and berries and chocolate sauce.

"Wow," said Sara. "You really did want to be a chef, didn't you?"

Nate laughed. "Too much? I wanted to impress you a little bit."

She chuckled. "You succeeded. And not just with the food."

He set the desserts on the table and smiled. "Good. I'm glad." He took her hands in his, the coolness of fingers that had been holding chilled desserts seemed to burn with tingling fire. "I wanted to say how much I've enjoyed getting to know you recently. I'm glad you came to Kowhiowhio. I'm glad you're here, with me, tonight."

Sara's mouth suddenly felt very dry. Her voice came out in a strange, hoarse whisper. "So am I."

He leaned closer, and she felt his breath on her cheek for an instant and then, gently, his lips touched hers, warm and firm. A spark of electric thrill ran through her core, filling her with excitement. Her breath stopped and her heart fluttered like fairy wings in her chest. His arms slipped around her waist and held her close. Her own hands slipped around his back and up to his broad shoulders, feeling the play of muscle under his shirt.

After what seemed a much too short eternity, he straightened up. The cool night air brushed over her naked lips, tingling each millimetre his had touched.

"Mmmm," he said. "I've been wanting to do that all week."

"I'm glad you did," Sara said, finding her voice again. Her grandmother's words were ringing in her mind. *Get back on the horse.* Might as well go for it. "Very glad."

She stepped up to his body and pressed herself against him. Her breasts rubbed into his chest, nipples hard and rough. She slipped her hands under his shirt, one sliding up over the skin of his back, the other down, into the waistband of his pants.

Nate's whole body went stiff. "Um…" he said.

Sara jerked back, her hands flying to her mouth. "Oh God. You don't want to." She stepped backward, putting the table between them. "Oh, I'm such an idiot. I'm sorry."

Nate reached out as if to touch her but she was too far away. "It's not that. I like you a lot. A heck of a lot. But Abi is in the house and there hasn't been anyone since Emma and…I just thought…maybe if we take things slower?”

Sara shut her eyes, feeling her cheeks flame hot. “Of course. Of course. Abigail could wake up and…God, I wasn’t thinking.” She shook her head. Stupid! She was so stupid.

“It’s okay.” Nate said. “No big deal.”

“I should go,” Sara said. She picked up her wine glass and gulped down the last of the liquid.

“There’s really no need…”

“It’s late and you have a daughter who will wake you up early tomorrow.” Somehow his being nice about it just made her embarrassment worse. She swooped in and gave him a peck on the cheek as she passed. “Thank you for everything. It was a wonderful night.”

And before he could say or do anything else, she ran out into the darkness and all the way home.

CHAPTER SIXTEEN

20 June, 1835

I think I've finally gotten my sea legs now. After two weeks, I feel like a salty sea-dog. The rest of the family are still feeling seasick when the wind is high, but I've been well for quite some time. Poor Father and Nan have it the worst. Jereth says I'm a natural with the elements.

The ship is starting to smell somewhat now. Our cabins are very basic but they're the best we could afford without looking suspicious. Nana and Jereth both agree that using the wrong sort of gold could get us thrown overboard. No captain likes to find his currency has turned to leaves.

Our supply of fresh fruit and vegetables has expired so the rest of the journey will be dried meat, pickles and what potatoes survive the damp of the hold. Today's dinner was stewed cabbage and salted beef. Not the most appetising of meals. I've offered to help the ship's cook where I can. I think it's best for a woman to be well liked by the crew if she can't keep her distance and I've no intention of spending this entire voyage in my cabin.

Jereth showed me a pod of dolphins this morning. They swam alongside the boat for almost an hour before vanishing beneath the waves. He really is quite handsome. I know there are stories about his people but I can't help thinking Jereth is different. He has a kind face, I think. I have a feeling about him.

"Don't we all." Sara rolled her eyes. "It always starts with the bloody feelings and next thing you know, your brain is out the window." She sighed, screwed up her nose, and flipped over a few pages before forcing her brain back to the written words.

29 June, 1835

Wonderful day. Warm and sunny with just a few clouds. Jereth asked the ship's cook for some food and made a picnic on the deck for us. The dolphins came back and we watched them together as the waves went by. Jereth had arranged for one of the sailors who has some little skill with the flute to play for us while we ate. I felt like a proper lady sailing a luxury barge down the river. It was wonderful.

15 July 1835

We will arrive in our new land of New Zealand in just a few days. I do not know what I will do when we are back on land and Jereth and I are back under the watchful eye of my family. The sailors have been so kind to us, protecting our love from prying eyes throughout the journey and allowing it to bloom. Jereth has given me a token of his intent. A beautiful ring crafted by his own hand. Even I, with my crude senses, know it is more than simple gemstones and promise. He has given me a great gift and I will treasure it always. For now, I can but keep it close to my heart until we have convinced both of our families to allow us to wed.

"And you didn't fuck it up by throwing yourself at him with his seven year old child in the next room? Well done."

Sara hurled the book onto the table. It hit the polished wood with a satisfying slap.

Hard as she tried to bury her tumultuous thoughts and feelings in her efforts to follow the bidding of the ghost, it was impossible. It'd been more than a day since the incredibly awkward ending to what had started out as a lovely first date with Nate Adams. She hadn't heard from him in that time, but, to be honest, she hadn't expected to. He wasn't working on Sunday so there was no need for Abigail to come over and no reason for him to come without his daughter being there.

This being Monday, however, that reprieve was coming to an end.

She felt incredibly stupid. Yet again. What was it about this man that had her making a fool of herself over and over in his presence? Had she been out of the dating world so long that she couldn't read the signs anymore? One moment she was certain it wasn't even a date, the next she'd thrown herself at the man. No wonder he was keeping his distance!

She sighed. There was no point worrying about it now. Best to keep her mind occupied. Well, as occupied as she could manage.

Whatever Bridget's ghost had hoped to share with her via this diary, Sara was sure she hadn't found it. Thus far it was simply the musings of a young girl on her way to a new country, falling in love on the boat. Lots of detail about the weather and the food and the various and fine qualities possessed by the young man known as Jereth, but very little that would indicate why the girl who wrote it would have wound up haunting this house.

"What am I missing?" Sara asked the empty room. There was no answer.

She sighed and glanced at her watch. The hands were still, the battery dead once more.

"Dammit, Bridget," she muttered. The realisation there was a ghost in the house had finally provided an explanation for all of the strange electrical problems she'd been having. Or perhaps the ghost was trying to give her a reason to talk to Nate again. Where else would she get a fresh battery in this small town?

She pushed up from the table and paced the house. Whatever the time was, Abigail should have been here by now. Had Nate decided she was too crazy after all and kept his daughter back? Or worse, had something happened to the girl on the way here?

She hurried to the window and peered out. The yard and the gravel road were empty. "Where is she?"

Dizziness swept over her, like a splashing wave on a boat bow, overwhelming then gone. Sara gasped and stumbled. As the wave passed, she turned back to the room expecting to see the ghost. "Bridget?"

A small glowing light spread out from the wall, oozing from one of the newly installed electrical sockets. It formed a buzzing orb, like the will-o'-the-wisp she'd followed into the bush days earlier. It hovered in the room over the couch for a long moment, then drifted toward the door.

Almost without thinking, Sara took a few steps after it. "What is that? Bridget? Is Abigail okay?"

The light pulsed and began moving faster.

"Shit." Sara followed it out onto the porch and watched it float around the side of the house, towards the bush. It followed the same path the earlier one had followed. The path that led to the circular pool.

A jolt of panic ran through her. A pool of water. If Abigail had gone wandering in the bush, the little girl could easily have fallen in.

She jumped the stairs and ran. Ahead of her, the will-o'-the-wisp vanished into the trees. Sara pelted after it as quickly as she could, leaping over small bushes and fallen logs as she went. Ferns and branches whipped at her body as she ran, but she ignored it.

Up ahead, the glowing ball suddenly stopped dead.

Sara slowed down as she approached it, puzzled. The ball gave a little hiccup and split apart into sparks that fell to the ground and vanished into the damp earth.

As her ragged breath calmed she heard a voice up ahead. A woman's voice, chanting in a sing-song rhythm.

"What the hell?"

She walked forward, peering through the trees and

out into the clearing with the circular pool. Sure enough, there was Abigail. The little girl was safe and sound, sitting on the edge on one of the stones around the pool, cross legged.

A woman stood over her, chanting words Sara couldn't understand. She recognised the language as te reo maori, but not the vocabulary. Her knowledge was limited at best.

The water in the pool glowed with phosphorescence, throwing swirling shadows across both adult and child. The tree in the centre quivered, leaves rustling.

As Sara watched, the woman stopped her incantation and the light in the water died. The tree became still. The woman turned to face Abi and Sara gasped as her face came into view. It was Moana.

"Did you memorise the *ripa* that time?" Moana said.

Abi shook her head, looking miserable.

Moana grabbed her by the elbow and pulled her to her feet. "You need to learn it! What if something happened to me like what happened to your mother? You have to pay attention!"

"It's hard!" Abi squirmed. "Ow! Auntie, let go. I have to go to Sara's house. Daddy said so. I'll get in trouble."

Moana let go and Abi fell backward onto the grass. "With Sara here, we're already in trouble."

"You certainly are," Sara called out, striding into the clearing. "What the hell do you think you're doing?"

Moana's eyes widened. "W-What are you doing here?"

"It's my property. What are you doing here? Aside from terrorising a little girl?"

Moana tugged her jacket tighter around herself. "Leaving," she said. As she passed Sara, she leaned in close. "I know what you are, O'Neill. My sister might be gone but I'm still here. I'll do whatever needs to be done to stop you. *Kauwaka.*"

And then she was gone, leaving Sara open mouthed and staring, Abigail at her feet.

CHAPTER SEVENTEEN

It took almost twenty minutes to get Abigail sufficiently settled after her aunt's tirade to make the journey back to the house. Even then, the little girl was strangely silent as they crossed the threshold. She dropped her pink backpack on the floor and wandered into the kitchen.

Sara followed. "Abi? You okay?"

"Yeah." The little girl helped herself to a glass of water while Sara watched. Then she sat down at the table.

Sara sat across from her. "Abi, what was your aunt doing in the bush?"

"I don't know." Abigail shrugged and stared at her drink. "Auntie Moana doesn't like you."

"I know. Do you know why?"

"No." She looked up, her dark brown eyes glistening. "I like you, though, Sara. You're much nicer than Auntie Moana."

Sara struggled to muffle her chuckle. "Thank you. I like you too." She pushed some scrap paper and coloured pencils across the table. "Maybe you could take these into the other room and draw me a picture of what you and your aunt were up to?"

"Okay." The little girl got down from the table, grabbed the drawing materials, and wandered into the hall.

Sara sat back with a sigh. She replayed what she'd seen over and over in her mind. The chanting incantation, the glow in the water, the shivering tree. Moana's insistence that Abigail learn the words and her vehement anger at Sara herself. This was more than a clash of personality or a proud townswoman's dislike of an old building. This was…strange.

"'I know what you are'," she muttered, repeating some of Moana's last words. "*'Kauwaka.'* Where have I heard *kauwaka* before?"

Her eyes fell on the journal. She sat upright. That was it! Fingers trembling, she flicked through the pages. It was toward the back. The first entry she'd read. Something the local iwi had said.

The words jumped out at her from the page. "*We were visited by the local Maori again today. This time they brought their Kuia. I think she's a wise woman, much like Nan. She spoke about our work in the forest and told us they believe what we are doing is dangerous. She called Nan and I kauwaka, and said we were fooling with things that are sacred and should not be touched.*"

What the hell had Bridget and her Nan been doing in the forest?

Sara set down the journal and picked up her smartphone. "Leave the damn battery alone this time, Bridget," she muttered, and pressed the button. A sigh of relief softened her mouth as the screen lit up. She flicked to the browser and found an online Maori to English dictionary site. She typed in the word and hit search, holding her breath as the signal connected to the network.

"Kauwaka," she read. "Human medium of an atua or spirit." She frowned. "Isn't *Atua* God?"

She typed the new word in to the search box and waited for the translation. A chill crept over her as she read the answer. "God, spirit, supernatural being…or demon."

Sara felt the hairs on her arms rise. She'd seen Bridget's ghost. If Moana thought she was a medium, it could be due to that. But the journal said the Maori in her lifetime had called Bridget a *kauwaka*. There had been no ghost here then. Bridget had been alive.

She read the definitions again, her heart pounding. Was she a human medium for a ghost? Or for something else?

CHAPTER EIGHTEEN

"Sara! Sara!" It was a piercing call, full of a little girl's panic and accompanied by the clatter of feet on the floorboards.

Sara jumped, her adrenaline already on high alert. The urgency in Abigail's voice stabbed into her like demon horns. "Abi? What's wrong?"

Abigail burst into the room, eyes wide. She scattered several coloured pencils in her wake and grasped Sara's sleeve. "Come quick! I think he's hurt."

"What? Who?"

She followed the little girl up the hallway, toward the back of the house. They stopped when they reached the red stickered rooms that had been declared unsafe by the building inspectors.

"He's in there. Listen."

Sara waited, straining her ears. A scratching sound came from within the wall ahead. Then a plaintive meow.

"See?" Abi's eyes were wide and tearful. "It's Oscar."

Sara felt her stomach sink. The meow came again. There was definitely a cat in the wall. She frowned. How the hell had the kitten gotten in? "Are you sure it's Oscar, Abi? Did you see him? A lot of stray cats like to hang around here."

The little girl's lip trembled. "No. But I can hear him, Sara. He's always coming over to your house. He's such a naughty cat."

"He is," Sara muttered. "Don't worry. He got himself in there. I'm sure he can get himself out."

But when Nate arrived to pick up his daughter that afternoon, it was obvious the cat was not going to find its way out of the wall. The meowing had become near constant yowls, punctuated by bursts of frantic scratching.

"We have an issue," Sara said as Nate arrived. "I need your help."

"I don't think it's structural," said Nate after a quick read of the inspector's report and checking of the wall. "We could knock a hole in it without too much trouble if you're okay with that."

Sara nodded, her vision caught on the sobbing girl in the hallway. "Let's do it. I was thinking of reworking a lot of this part of the house anyway. Let's get him out."

Nate fetched a sledge hammer and a crowbar from his ute and together they attacked the wall. Chips of faded wallpaper and semi-rotted wood fell like hailstones, then Nate used the crowbar to pry away a big chunk of the wall and they peered inside.

The cat was gone.

Sara chewed her lip. "Do you think he found his way out or has he just crawled further back to get away from us?"

Nate shrugged. "Got a torch?"

Sara held up her phone, flicked on the flashlight app, and shone it into the hole. Beyond was a larger space than she'd expected. This section of the house was the intersection of three walls and had created a kind of alcove, sealed off from the house itself – like a cupboard space with no door to provide access. It smelled of dust and damp stone and was filled with cobwebs. There was no sign of Abi's kitten but…

"Are those stairs?" Nate peered over Sara's shoulder.

She angled the light. Sure enough, a spiral stone staircase circled downward. "It must lead to the basement. I knew there was one but I never found it."

Nate raised an eyebrow. "Shall we investigate?"

Sara felt her lips twitch upward. "Let's!"

It didn't take long to widen the hole enough to squeeze through it and, with Sara's phone in torch mode still and Abigail given strict instructions to stay put, Nate and Sara made their way down the stairs, carefully testing each one before putting weight on it.

The light from the phone threw shadows across the walls. The stairs were narrow, steep, and grey with dust and mouse droppings. The air was cool and smelled of stone and old damp wallpaper. Sara felt cobwebs cling to her hair as she descended. She tried not to think about the possibility of spiders crawling over her skin.

She shook her head to shake them off.

"You okay?" Nate's voice was rich and comforting, like the first sip of coffee in the morning. It filled her with a warm glow.

"Yeah." Sara took a deep breath. "Hey, I'm sorry about the other night. I hope you weren't offended by me…you know."

Nate chuckled. "Not at all. It was flattering. Although, that is twice now that you've basically sprinted out of my house when you visit. You'll notice I don't do that when I come over. I take my time and climb into dark dungeons with you and say goodbye and stuff."

She slapped his shoulder playfully. "Smart arse. I was embarrassed."

He flashed her a smile. "You don't have to be. I like you. Quirks and all."

Sara was glad of the darkness that hid her flaming cheeks. "I like you too."

The stairs opened out into a wide area with a stone block floor. Chinks of light crept in from the floorboards overhead, accenting more than mitigating the darkness.

Sara held up her phone and the light bored into the shadow.

"What the hell?" Nate whistled.

The basement was a single room, almost the size of the entire house. Strange, stiff vines criss-crossed the entire room. They stuck out of the walls and ceiling, stabbing across the room in straight lines, like some kind of laser beam security grid with leaves. Some of them sliced all the way to the other side of the room and vanished into the opposing surface like giant spears. Others intersected, twisted around each other, then continued in a different direction.

Sara reached out to touch the one closest to her. It was hard and cold. "It's stone."

"Really?" Nate tapped one himself. "Why? What's it supposed to be?"

"I don't know." Sara moved forward, turning to take in the room. It was like being in some kind of haphazard spider web or a fossilized jungle tree house tied together by Tarzan. And that was it, she realized. The vines *did* tie something together. "It's the mantelpiece motif."

Nate frowned. "What?"

"On the fireplace upstairs. It has vines carved into the mantle. If you look around the house, it's everywhere. Well, the older parts of it anyway. There are vines on everything. I was going to use them as part of the restoration."

"And these are, what? Left over carvings they stuck in the basement? Some sort of art installation?"

"No, it's more than that." Sara shook her head. This wasn't a haphazard placement of stone carvings. There was something to it. Something she couldn't quite put her finger on. "Bridget? Did you do this?"

There was no response from the ghost.

"Who's Bridget?" asked Nate.

"One of the people who built the house." She traced a finger over the nearest vine, following it deeper into the room. There was no dust, no grime, just smooth, cool stone. "This is the heart of it," she said. "The heart of the house."

"I'd always heard that was the kitchen." Nate's tone was dry as he followed her into the web of vines, just a few steps behind.

"Not this one." Sara could feel something drawing her forward, calling to her. There was a pattern to the stone vines. A thickening of their intersections the further into the middle of the room she went. After a few steps, she had to duck and weave to get past the stone foliage. At last, she reached its core – a thicket of vines producing a kind of cabinet of stone in the centre of the room, and, she suspected, the centre of the house itself.

"Here it is." She reached into the opening left by the tangled vines, her fingers touching, feeling around, seeking. Something warm and furry brushed against her.

She yelped and jumped back.

A low rumbling noise emanated from the space. Two shining green eyes peered out of the darkness.

"What is it?" Nate hurried forward.

Sara sneezed. "I think I found Oscar." She reached back in and pulled out the kitten. He snuggled into to her, purring even louder.

Nate chuckled. "Well that's something."

Sara handed the kitten over to him and turned back to the vine cabinet. "There's something else. This is here for a reason, I know it." She reached into the space again. This time her fingers closed on something hard and rounded. "Got it."

"Got what?"

"This." She drew her hand back out of the gap and held up a stone water lily. The only blossom on any vine in the entire house.

"A flower?" Nate was unimpressed.

"Look closer," said Sara. She'd already seen the tell-tale sparkle in the torchlight produced by her phone.

In the centre of the lily, hooked over the stamen, was a ring. She recognized it from the portrait in the hall.

"Bridget's engagement ring."

CHAPTER NINETEEN

"Abigail's gone." Nate's boots disappeared through the gap in the wall ahead of her. His words dropped into the hidden stairwell like a heavy weight.

"What?" Sara took the last few steps two at a time, ducked through the hole and out into the hallway. It was empty. "Nate? Where are you? What do you mean Abi's gone?"

He stepped out from around the corner, brandishing a note. "I just found this." Oscar, the kitten, wriggled in his other arm, but Nate held him close. After having spent so much effort to find and rescue the kitten, neither of them wanted to risk letting him go again just yet.

Sara took the note. "Found Abigail here alone. Am taking her with me. Moana."

"This is typical." Nate's jaw was tight. "Abigail must have told her we were just downstairs. Why would she take her out of the house without telling us?"

Sara scowled at the note. "It's me. She doesn't like me."

"Well that's no excuse. I'm Abigail's father. I'm the one who makes the decisions about what's best for her. Not her aunt."

"It sounds like she was just worried about her. I'm sure they're okay." Sara was vaguely surprised to find herself standing up for Moana.

"That's not the point," Nate said. "She wasn't in any danger and she should have talked to me before taking her away. Now I have to figure out where they've gone."

Sara thought about where she'd found Abigail and her aunt earlier that day. "I think I may have an idea. How about I check there and you check the house in case she just took her home?"

Nate nodded. "Thanks. Sorry about this. I'll call you and let you know if they're there."

As soon as he was gone, Sara pulled on her shoes and hurried outside and into the bush. This time there was no glowing light to guide her, but she knew the way to the circular pond now. As she pushed her way through the ferns and branches, she questioned why she was headed there again. Surely Moana wouldn't return to the same place so soon?

But then, Sara had no real idea what the woman had been doing there in the first place. She'd already practically kidnapped the girl and taken her there once today. The knowledge that it had been done without Nate's permission ate at Sara. Somehow it hadn't felt right to tell Nate what she'd seen and yet, now that she was hurrying to the pond again, there was a heaviness in her stomach that seemed like guilt.

Why hadn't she told him? The question rang in her

ears with every step.

The answer was fear.

Nate had been so nice to her, so accepting of her situation and her past. She liked him – a lot – and she felt that he liked her. He'd even said so as they'd explored the hidden staircase. To mention what she'd seen opened all sorts of doors. Nate had accepted her abusive relationship and lost baby, but would he accept her talking about ghosts and magic and accusing his sister-in-law of chanting spells in the bush with his daughter?

Wasn't that the kind of thing that sent decent men running? At best, he would think she was crazy. At worst… did small towns still gather up mobs with pitchforks these days?

She reached the clearing and felt a wash of relief go through her. There was no sign of Moana and Abigail. Most likely, the woman had simply taken the girl home.

Sara walked closer, peering at the water. There was no sign of what had made it glow earlier in the day, the only living creature other than herself was one of the neighbourhood cats resting on one of the stones at the edge of the water. She'd hoped perhaps some kind of natural algae could explain what she'd seen while Moana was chanting, but no. There was something supernatural at work here and something told her it was more than just Bridget's ghost.

Her hand in her pocket fingered the engagement ring she'd found in the basement.

The water in the pool rippled and the tree in its centre shifted as though in the wind. It was almost as though the branches were reaching out to her. As she watched, she felt something inside her stir, as if some creature in her stomach had come to life. The perfume of flowers wafted over her, but there were none nearby that she could see. The water shimmered in the light like stars captured beneath the water from another world.

"Closer," a man's deep voice said inside her head. "Come closer and help us."

His voice was like a hook in her chest and she took a step forward before she even thought about what she was doing.

The cat on the rock looked up suddenly and hissed.

Sara shook her head and the spell was broken. She backed away, heart pounding, and hurried back to the house.

CHAPTER TWENTY

Her allergies were playing up by the time she reached the house again. Another couple of stray cats were on the porch. She sneezed as she passed them, her hands slapping her thighs with the violence of it.

The lump in her pocket was Bridget's engagement ring.

She took out the ring and held it up to the sunlight. The stone sparkled, almost as if it created its own light. It really was beautiful. What had it been doing in the basement all this time? Who had left it there and why?

There were just too many questions and not enough answers.

She stepped across the threshold and her gaze caught on a small pink backpack tucked up against the hall table.

"Abi? Are you here?"

There was no response. The little girl must have left it behind when Moana had taken her from the house. A quick check of her cell-phone revealed a text from Nate saying he'd found Abigail and Moana at his house and not to worry.

Sara felt a weight lift from her. At least they hadn't gone far. Whatever power struggle Nate and Moana had, it wasn't her business. They had to figure out how to look after Abigail between them.

Nevertheless, Sara couldn't help the niggle of concern that felt like a cold worm in her throat. She'd started to care for Abigail. She'd seen enough tug-of-war parenting at the child care facility to know how confusing it could be for a child.

She stared at the backpack for a long moment. Perhaps she should take it over to Nate and Abigail's house and just make sure everything was all right.

She slipped Bridget's ring onto her finger, for safe keeping, and bent down to pick up the backpack.

A rushing sound, like a river pouring through a dark cave, echoed through her mind. The world fell away and Sara spiralled into a swirl of blinding light, losing herself as her senses were overwhelmed. She screamed and fought it, but for a long moment, nothing happened. Then, slowly, the light and the noise subsided.

The hallway was gone. The light shrank down to a spark of brightness, a gemstone on a woman's hand. Bridget's hand.

They stood in a wide, stone room, empty of furniture. Bridget was surrounded by a circle of Maori women, each with a tattooed *moko* on her chin. As the glowing ring on Bridget's finger pulsed with light, the women began to sing.

Bridget's face was a grimace of concentration. From the walls and floor, long stone spikes lanced out, each one sprouting leaves as it went, creating a lattice of vines throughout the room. Showers of sparks sprayed out wherever the vines connected.

One of the Maori women screamed as sparks danced over her skin and she fell to the ground. The others closed ranks, singing their chant louder and stronger than before.

As their voices blended in crescendo, Bridget opened her mouth to speak.

Sara hit the floor, pain jolting through her shoulder in a shocking burst.

The vision was gone. She was back in the hallway, her face resting against Abigail's little pink backpack.

Sara pushed herself up from the floor, her legs wobbly and her head spinning.

Her stomach was tight with fear, adrenaline rushing through her veins. "Bridget?" she called.

But the ghost gave no response.

"Damn it, Bridget. What are you? What's happening to me?" Whatever supernatural things were happening in the house and at the pond in the bush, were affecting her as well. The magic of this place was overwhelming and it was beginning to frighten her.

She took a deep breath, picked up the pink backpack, and hurried out the door.

CHAPTER TWENTY-ONE

Nate's stomach felt as though he'd swallowed a live wire as he bounded up the steps to his front door. The keys felt like tiny sharp knives in his fingers as he struggled to get the right one in the lock. At last, the door opened and he stepped inside.

"Abi? You here?"

Moana and his daughter sat at the dining table, colouring in. Abi looked up and smiled at the kitten in his arms.

"Yay! You found him!" She scrambled down and took the small cat. Nate quickly shut the door so the creature wouldn't escape again.

"Of course she's here," Moana said blandly. "Where else would I take her? Or has that O'Neill woman been filling your head with nonsense?"

Nate felt his jaw twitch with annoyance, but the surge of relief that soothed his chest took the main part of his focus. It was foolish to have thought any harm would come to Abigail while she was with her aunt, but ever since Emma's death, it was hard to let go of certain fears. He hated not knowing where his daughter was. Hated the feeling of helplessness that came from having his power as a parent taken away.

He took a deep breath. "I'm going to make a cup of tea." He put the jug on and pulled out his phone to text Sara so she wouldn't worry. "Abi, Hon, why don't you take Oscar to your room for a while."

She looked at him, then at her aunt. Her eyes narrowed slightly but she picked up the kitten and walked slowly to the door. Nate sighed. The older Abi got, the harder it was to hide the friction in the family from her.

Moana stared at him, her jaw lifted.

Nate folded his arms and stared back. "What the hell were you thinking, taking my daughter without asking?"

"What was I thinking? What were you thinking? I found her alone in a dangerously unstable house. Anything could have happened to her."

The jug boiled and he poured hot water into the cup. "She was not alone. Sara and I were downstairs. Aside from the fact that I doubt you had permission to be inside the house at all, if you'd left Abi alone, she'd have stayed where she was safe, just as I'd told her. You can't make decisions about her without consulting me. You're not her parent. I am."

"Well you could have fooled me about that when Emma died." Moana's voice was soft and dark. "Or have you forgotten the weeks on end that I was the one who fed and washed and dressed your daughter? That I would walk in here and find you sitting in a corner with dirty dishes all around you, stained clothes, and no interest in the world at all? Let alone your daughter's wellbeing."

"I always cared about my daughter's wellbeing," Nate snapped. "Always. But I had just lost my wife and I had a hard time dealing with it. I know that. I'm grateful for your help back then. But damn it, Moana, that was years ago! You have to let it go! I know how to raise my daughter now."

She looked at him and raised her eyebrow. "Do you?"

Doubt stabbed at his chest. He knew so little about girls. "Maybe not. Maybe I'm making some mistakes. But I'm doing the best I can and they're my mistakes to make, not yours. For me to be the best parent I can be, I need to do it my way and you need to stop undermining me. Let me do it."

She was silent for a while. Then she stood up, walked across and made herself a cup of tea as well, pouring milk into his cup and pushing it towards him. "Perhaps. But there are some things I still need to help you with. For Abigail's sake."

"Like what?"

"The traditions of our people," she said. "And female issues, when she's older."

Nate nodded. He felt some of the tension leave his shoulders. "Sure. An aunt would be great for that. But talk to me about it first, okay?" He lifted the cup of tea to his mouth.

Moana pursed her lips. "I will try," she said. "But you shouldn't be leaving her with that woman. Abi needs a firm hand and you're letting her run wild. She can't learn what she needs to with her."

The tension in his shoulders returned, muscles twisting into painful knots. "With Sara, you mean? Why on earth not? She's probably the best person to babysit. She's an early childhood education teacher for God's sake."

"That's not all she is."

Nate frowned and set the cup down. "What do you mean by that?"

Moana shook her head. "She's an O'Neill. That's all you need to know. They can't be trusted."

"Why?"

"They just can't."

He sighed. "You know, Moana, for someone who is so involved in her iwi and biculturalism, I thought you'd be more accepting than that. Hating someone just for their family is basically the same as racism. You've never really given her a chance."

She looked away. "You don't know what you're talking about."

"Then by all means, explain it."

"You're a newcomer to this town as well. You don't know the history of this place. Of that house."

"I thought nobody had lived there for a couple of generations now. Whatever happened, you can't blame Sara for it."

Moana traced the rim of her cup with a finger. "What did she say about me?"

Nate sighed. "Nothing. I mean, I don't think she particularly likes you, but that's because you're trying to have her house torn down."

"So she said nothing about why she has come back here now? About what her family did when they settled in our land?"

Nate shook his head. "No. Why would she? What are you even on about? Why does it matter what happened a hundred years ago?"

Moana snorted. "Emma never spoke to you about this at all, did she? Damn her for being such a cagey bitch."

"Excuse me?" Nate felt his fingers curl into fists. "That's your dead sister you're talking about. My dead wife."

Moana rolled her eyes. "Oh please. You think I didn't know her at least as well as you did? Do you think it was a coincidence that she wanted you to live here, right next to the O'Neill house all these years? That she always talked you out of moving back to the city? Did you honestly never wonder where she went on her big long bush walks alone?"

"What are you talking about?" A worm of dread bit into his stomach. Emma had been the one to choose this house. She'd always wanted to stay in her home town. He'd always thought it was cute. That it was a sign of feeling like she belonged to this town and this land. That home meant something special to her and that her position in the iwi was important. She'd said it was a good place to raise their children and so he'd stayed even after she'd died. But what if there was more? "What do you mean?"

Moana leaned forward, her eyes narrowed. "There's a reason Emma was a *kuia* so young. She had a hereditary job to do. Her role was to maintain the gateway to *rarohenga*, to the spirit world. Every month she went into the bush and performed a *ripa* to keep the gateway closed. Our family has done this for generations. We are the keepers of that gate. We have to protect this land and keep the thing the O'Neills brought with them trapped. That's what your wife was doing. That's why she was in such a damn hurry to get home when she died."

"But…how did you know?" Nate had never told anyone that Emma had been speeding when her car was hit by the truck. He'd never wanted her family to think less of her or feel angry at her over the accident.

Moana snorted. "I found out everything I could when she died. I hoped she would have prepared in case something happened to her. She was the only one who knew how to…" Her voice trailed off.

"So you invaded our privacy for your superstitions," Nate said. It was hard to keep the anger out of his voice.

"They're not superstitions," Moana insisted. Her finger stabbed at the air in front of her. "That family brought something unnatural to New Zealand with them and we've kept it trapped ever since. But a lot of our knowledge died with Emma. Abigail and I are the only ones left to maintain the gate now. We have to stop that O'Neill woman from releasing a dangerous *atua*."

"Are you serious? You're picking on an innocent, lovely woman because of a family myth? And you want to teach my daughter to do the same?" His skin felt hot and prickly.

"She's far from innocent," Moana said. "She and all her kind are a freak of nature and should never have been allowed here. Her ancestors brought the creature with them when they came here and her presence has awakened it. Without my sister's knowledge, our ways are weakened but we must stop it breaking free. I will do what must be done."

Nate stared at her. "You're crazy," he said. "And you will leave my daughter and Sara O'Neill alone if you know what's good for you."

Moana was breathing hard. Her eyes wild. "She's bewitched you!" Spittle flew from her lips as she spoke. "You're a fool if you think she hasn't. She's a dangerous freak and should never have been allowed to come back to Kowhiowhio."

Nate drew himself up to his full height. "I don't care what kind of freak she is. I'll not have you spreading such lies about someone I care about. And I certainly won't have you filling Abigail's head with this nonsense. Sara O'Neill has had a very hard life up 'til now. She's lost a child and she's been abused. She does not need your bullshit monster stories making her life worse."

Moana opened her mouth to answer but he cut her off.

"You need to get out of my house, Moana. Now."

The woman's dark eyes widened in shock, but she quickly covered it and haughtily picked up her coat. "Oh, I'll go," she said. "But you mark my words. If your new girlfriend sets free the creature her ancestors brought with them, it won't just be her life that gets worse. Our whole country will suffer." She stalked to the door and paused on the threshold. "There will be more deaths at that O'Neill house, Nate. You just see if there aren't." Then she disappeared outside.

Nate frowned, a chill in his chest at her words. "What do you mean by that, Moana?" He called after her. When there was no answer, he followed her outside. She was already disappearing down the road. “Moana? What did you mean by that?”

She ignored him and kept walking.

Nate sighed and turned to go back into the house and his eyes caught sight of something pink on the steps. It was Abigail’s backpack.

“Oh God.” A jolt ran through him. The backpack hadn’t been there when he’d arrived. There was only one person who could have dropped it off. He ran to the gate and looked in the other direction, towards the O’Neill house. “Sara? Sara!”

She ignored him as well, her slim figure disappearing into the overgrown grass.

“Damn it!” He swore and kicked the ground. How much had she heard?

Enough to be offended, of that much he was sure. He sighed and went back inside to his daughter.

CHAPTER TWENTY-TWO

Sara slammed the door behind her and leaned on it. She closed her eyes and took a deep breath. Nate's words played over in her mind. He'd called her a freak and told Moana about her past. Why had she been stupid enough to tell him about her history with Greg and the baby? How could she start fresh if people here all knew about her past and talked about it behind her back?

She sighed, pushed off from the door and walked slowly down the hall. It served her right for eavesdropping. Not that she'd intended to hear their argument. She'd only paused a moment to see if it was a good time to drop off Abigail's backpack. It was old instinct to gauge the state of the people in a room before entering. Raised voices or a feeling of rage had always meant danger with Greg.

Nate was a completely different man to her ex. She knew that. But still she'd run away from him like a scared little girl and made a fool of herself once again.

"Typical," she muttered.

As she walked into the dining room a flicker of movement caught her eye. Bridget's ghost stood by the table, her form transparent, but her face stern. The journal lay in front of her, open.

Sara started, her heart tight in her chest. She took a deep breath to calm herself and faced the ghost. "You again. I thought you were ignoring me."

Transparent arms raised up towards her and the pages of the journal fluttered as if in a strong breeze. "Beware." The ghost's whispery voice sent shivers up Sara's spine. "Do not trust him."

A surge of annoyance ran through her. Distrust was not something she needed lessons in. "Who? Nate? Listen, just because your relationship went belly up, doesn't mean I need you spooking over my shoulder, messing up mine." She looked away for a moment and bit her lip. "Not that my track record is any better," she admitted.

"Read my words," said Bridget.

The journal pages settled.

Sara reached across the table and pulled the book towards her. "To be honest, there hasn't been that much of interest in here so far."

"Read." Bridget's image pulsed, almost tangible for an instant, then back to transparency once more.

"Fine, fine." Sara gritted her teeth and looked at the journal. The words seemed to jump off the page at her.

I'm so scared of what Jereth will do to me. The power he displayed in the forest was terrifying. He will kill us all if he gets the chance, I know he will. I can't believe I was ever foolish enough to think he loved me. All of his kind are cruel and deceitful and violent. How could he be any different?

Sara pulled her eyes away from the page. She recognized the emotion in those words all too well. The fear. Fear of a man that she loved. Bridget had gone through the same kind of terror that she herself had experienced with Greg.

"Read," said the ghost. She was closer now, standing next to Sara, pointing at the book.

"No." Sara shook her head and stepped back. This was why she'd left everything behind. This was why she'd refused the counsellor's offer of a support group or women's refuge. There was no way she wanted to relive someone else's experience of terror and abuse at the hands of a man. She could barely keep clear of her own. It had taken her years to leave it behind. She could not – would not – take on more.

"Read," demanded Bridget. The journal pages fluttered again, like a frightened bird's wings in a cage.

"No!" Sara felt all the anger, all the rage, all the humiliation of her life with Greg come rushing up from the depths of her soul like some tsunami of emotion. She would not be bullied any more. She would make her own decisions. She'd had enough of living in fear. "Enough! If you have something you want me to know, then tell me. Show me!"

She thrust out her hand to push the other woman back. Her arm passed through the ghost's form, a chill tingle on her skin. The engagement ring she still wore on her finger burned hot and light spread out from the gemstone.

Bridget screamed.

CHAPTER TWENTY-THREE

The colours of the room melted together then spread glowing sparks of light in cascading showers. Sara's arm tingled as though she'd gripped hold of an electric fence and couldn't let go. Bridget's screams echoed in her head, louder and louder, then, abruptly, they were gone.

The spill of colours resolved into a scene of two women in the woods. Sara knew somehow that she was watching memories.

The women were hunched down in a circular clearing, marked by smooth river stones. One was an old woman, her grey hair tied back in a bun. The other was young, perhaps nineteen or so. When she turned her face slightly, Sara realized it was Bridget, decades before her death, in the prime of youth. Several cats were scattered around the clearing, drawn by the magic here. They lay in the grass or pounced on insects.

"Nan, are you sure this is a good idea?" The young Bridget fidgeted as they sat, waiting. Her voice as a living girl was much stronger than her ghost self and the

Irish accent thick. "You've always told me the fae were not to be trifled with."

The older woman nodded. "Aye, that's true. But you've heard your father. There's nothing left for us here. We're better to try our luck in a new part of the world and that's dangerous. If we can make a deal with the fair folk, we can gain their protection."

As Sara watched, a shimmer of light appeared in the centre of the circle. It expanded to the size of a doorway and then vanished, leaving behind a tall, incredibly beautiful man. His hair was golden and down to his shoulders, his eyes were green like oak leaves in spring. Vines and leaves wrapped around his limbs, climbed around his body and formed a crown on his brow. He held out a hand and a ball of twisting, crackling lightning formed there. He bounced it idly on his palm as he stared at the two women on the grass.

"Madam O'Neill," he said in a voice as deep and earthy as tree roots. "Why have you summoned me?"

The older woman stood and bowed her head in greeting. Bridget scooted backward a few steps. Sara could feel the shiver of awe that ran through the younger woman.

"My lord Jereth of the forest," Bridget's Nan began. "We are both of an old time and old ways but this world is beginning anew. My granddaughter and I wish to propose an arrangement between our family and yours, so that both our peoples can thrive in the new world."

The fae lord stared into the ball of lightning in his hand. "Why should I be concerned about what humans call a new world?"

The old woman shrugged. "Iron."

Jereth looked up sharply. "What about it?"

"There's too much of it in the world these days. Too much for both of us by far. Progress and industry are spreading iron and other metals throughout our country. Machines and electricity are taking jobs from honest men and the metal that goes with them are a problem for your kind's magic. There will be less iron in the new countries across the sea. Your people would be safe there. We could help you get there."

He tilted his head to one side. "An interesting proposal. What would you desire in return?"

"Protection for the trip," Bridget's Nana said. "And help establishing a new home. We want a fresh start. My son has no work here anymore."

Jereth laughed, a sound like a rockslide of precious stones. "And the people in your village have named you witch. They see the signs of magic around you. The cats that flock to your side, the parsley that grows like wildfire in your garden. They are afraid of you. This new, modern world is more dangerous for you than it is for us."

"Really?" The old woman pulled out a metal rod and stuck it point first into the earth. The ball of lightning leapt from Jereth's palm and struck the rod, sizzling into the dirt and burning the grass around it. "Iron hurts your powers. You fae manipulate energy and there's too much energy and iron in this new industrial world." She gestured to the circle of stones. "The fae can only enter the human world through these special portals and there are fewer and fewer of them all the time. Before long, you will be trapped in your own realm. Will that be enough for you? Denied the power and beauty of this world? I don't believe that it will be."

The fae lord scowled. "Perhaps."

"Protect me and my family on our journey to New Zealand and we will create a portal for you there. A circle in a new country. A fresh, unsullied country with no metal machines, no towns, and where yours is the only energy to be manipulated. It will be just like the old days for your kind."

Jereth looked from her to Bridget and back again. Sara felt the thrill in Bridget as the fae's gaze met hers. "Very well. I agree. I will come with you on your journey. We will work and create opportunity for us both in this new country you speak of. When do we leave?"

The scene split apart into sparks once more and swirled like embers in the wind. They reformed, creating shapes and figures. Bridget and Jereth, standing on the beach at sunset. Kauri and punga formed a backdrop in the dwindling sunlight. A large sailboat was at anchor in the bay and several longboats shared space with *waka* on the shore.

"We can't hide this from my family much longer," said Bridget. "There will be nowhere to hide when we begin building our new home."

Jereth nodded. "I know, my love. When the circle is created and I can speak to my people again, we will face them both together."

Bridget sighed. "Do you think it will be very difficult to convince them? Surely when they realize how much we care for each other…"

"I do not know, Bridget. All I know is that I will not live my life without you. The time we spent on that unbearable ship was crafted into a thing of beauty because of your presence. I never thought I would love a human, but now I cannot think of loving anyone but you." He pulled a ring from his pocket and held it out to her. "My dearest Bridget, I know I must get the permission of your family and my own, but first I must ask for your own heart. Will you wear my ring? Will you be my bride?"

Bridget clapped her hands together, her eyes wide and moist. Sara could feel the girl's elation. "Yes! Oh, of course, Jereth. Yes!"

He smiled, lips parting just enough to show canines more sharply pointed than most human's. "You have made me very happy, my love. When you wear this ring, know that it was made in a fae smithy and the gem is crafted in the other realm. It holds the key to my heart and my power. Wear it and I will be with you always. My magic is yours to command now, as well as your own. It is the best I can do to protect you from all harm."

"Thank you, my love." Bridget stood on her toes and kissed him.

Jereth slipped the ring onto her finger. Sparks fountained around them like sea spray and they laughed, a happy, delighted sound, and walked into the trees hand in hand.

The spray of sparks swirled again and the scene changed once more.

Bridget and her Nan dug into the earth, scooping handfuls of dirt with their bare hands. The pit was a perfect circle. When the rains came, it would fill with water. Saplings were already planted at the points of the compass and key-stones placed around the edge. The magic of the portal hummed just on the outer edge of the world, nearly close enough to touch.

As the sun came out from behind a cloud, something on Bridget's finger caught the light.

Her grandmother snatched her hand and rubbed away the dirt. "What's this?"

Bridget tried to pull her hand away, but the old woman's grip was strong.

"That's a fae ring. Did Jereth give you this?"

Bridget lifted her chin. "Yes."

Nan dropped her hand as if it burned. "What have I always told you about accepting gifts from fae? You fool. You have no idea what you've been bound to by taking it."

"But I love him." Bridget reached for her grandmother, pleading for her to understand. "And he loves me. We're going to be married. I wanted to tell you and Papa about it but Jereth needs to talk to his people first. Oh, Nan, I'm so happy!"

"Aye," the old woman snorted. "And the Spring lamb is happy 'til the knife's at his throat. You'd best keep that ring hidden from your father."

The sound of soft, ghostly sobs filled Sara's ears as her vision was again obscured by swirling sparks of light. "Bridget?" she called gently. "What happened?"

The ghost continued to cry as the sparks cleared and the younger Bridget paced on the porch. The wood of the house was unpainted, newly hewn and hammered into place, sanded carefully smooth. There was dirt under the girl's fingernails and she chewed on her lip and fiddled with the ring on her finger as she paced.

A young man sat on the porch steps and watched her, his face solemn. Sara somehow knew this was Bridget's brother. Neither of them noticed the ghost's sobs or Sara's presence.

An older man burst out of the bush, running at full speed toward the house. "Help! Get help. We are betrayed!"

Bridget froze. "Papa? What happened? Where's Jereth?"

Her father's face was red and wet with sweat. "Jereth betrayed us. He's killed your Nan and he's bringing an army of fae through the portal to destroy us all!"

"What?" Sara could feel the paralyzing cold in Bridget's veins. "No, Papa, no! He would never do such a thing!"

"See for yourself," her father snapped. "Your Nan slowed him down, but he's going to break free. Patrick, get the Maori woman. Now!"

The boy on the steps leapt to his feet and Bridget lurched forward. The scene dissolved into a blur of leaves as she ran, at last bursting out into the clearing with the portal.

In the centre of the circle, Jereth was frozen, half in and half out of the water, his body twisted and his beautiful face snarled with rage. Lightning crackled from his fist, spinning a web of burning power across the circle. It sizzled and twisted, making shadows dance among the trees. The water in the pool swirled around him. Lights like fireflies glowed beneath the surface.

"Jereth!" Bridget called. "What have you done?"

"What have I done?" His eyes flashed fire. "What

was necessary!"

She ran forward, her heart sinking in her chest. "Jereth, please stop."

Her foot struck something soft. She looked down. The still form of her Nan lay in the grass, her skin blackened with burn marks. She was dead.

"No. No!" The horror of it choked the words in her throat.

Jereth growled, his muscles straining against whatever held his lower half in the water, trapped in the realm on the other side. "Set me free, witch! Set me free!"

The lightning spilling from his skin trembled and flexed. A strand of it touched Bridget but she felt nothing. The ring on her finger glowed brightly, its power protecting her against his magic.

She stood up tall, wiped her eyes and squared her shoulders. She would not let this man, this murderer, this creature of fae deceive her again. "No!" She pointed her fist at the portal and the gemstone in the ring he'd given her flared bright. She drew on all the magic her Nan had taught her, everything of the Earth, and everything she could access of fae magic through the ring and flung it all at the fairy circle she and her grandmother had created, slamming it closed.

A blast of energy washed over the clearing and knocked her from her feet. She hit the ground in a painful thud that rattled her bones. When she looked up, Jereth was gone. In his place was a twisted, stunted kauri tree growing in the centre of the circle's pool.

A hand touched her shoulder and she gasped. When she turned, it was the older Maori woman, the one they called *kuia*. "You did well, girl," the old woman said kindly. Her *moko* was a dark pattern of ink against the brown of her skin. "It is done."

Bridget felt her eyes fill with tears. "Why?" she wailed. "Why did he do that? I loved him so much."

The *kuia* pulled her into an embrace. "I know, child. But he was a spirit creature. An *ira atua*. He did not belong in this place. You did right to shut the gate to his world."

"I don't think it will hold," Bridget choked out between sobs. "I couldn't force him back before I closed it. He's still half in our world. I think he'll escape."

The Maori woman lifted her chin with her hand, her dark eyes searched Bridget's, then, seemingly satisfied, she nodded. "Then we will help you keep him there. He must never be allowed into this world or he will kill us all."

CHAPTER TWENTY-FOUR

"Sara? Sara!" Something gripped her shoulder and shook her. Sara forced her eyes open and lashed out, slapping at the creature that was pulling her down.

"Get away from me!"

The fog cleared from her mind and she saw Nate backing away, his hands spread apart, palms up. There were three cats in the dining room, just casually washing or sitting watching her. Strangely, she didn't feel the urge to sneeze.

"I'm sorry," Nate said. "You were unconscious. I was worried."

Sara rubbed at her eyes. Her pulse was still pounding in her ears. Bridget's adrenaline still rushing through her veins. The visions had been so real. Memories. They *were* real. She couldn't explain it but she knew what she had seen really happened. Another betrayal from another man. Another woman heartbroken to pick up the pieces after a death.

Bridget's Nan, Sara's own unborn child. Would

there be no end to the heartbreak? Men weren't to be trusted. Any of them. They were all sweetness and light at the beginning but that light burned and it was Sara and those she loved who would pay the price for it.

Nate stepped forward and reached out to help her up.

"Back off!" she snapped, thrusting out her hand to stop him.

He staggered back a few steps as if he'd been pushed. "What's wrong?"

Sara pulled herself to her feet. "You tell me."

He sighed. "You overheard Moana and I. Listen, she has some strange superstitions. Don't let it get to you. It doesn't mean anything to me and I'm sure everyone else in town will ignore it too."

"You think I care what Moana thinks?" Sara steadied herself on the back of the chair. "I heard *you*, Nate. I trusted you and you told her I was a freak and you told her every secret I'd opened up to you about. How do you think that makes me feel?"

"I…" His mouth moved soundlessly for a moment. "I was trying to defend you. I didn't realize…"

"What? That my abusive ex and dead child weren't something I'd want everyone in town to know about? That I opened up to you about my deepest, darkest secrets because I care about you? Because I thought you cared about me and would be a safe person to talk to about it?" Her whole body was quivering with emotion. She gripped the back of the chair so hard her knuckles went white, determined not to let him see how much his betrayal had hurt her. "Don't you worry. I've learned my lesson. I learned it long ago. Reveal any weakness and people will use it against you. Greg always did. I just thought you were different."

Nate moved towards her, his arms wide. "Sara, I…"

Sara flinched.

Nate froze. His mouth dropped open. "My God. You thought I was going to hit you."

Sara stared at the floor. "I don't know. I don't know what I think any more."

"Wow." Nate closed his eyes and took a deep breath through his nose. "Wow. I think you know how I feel about you, Sara. I would never hit anyone I care about, no matter what they said to me. If you can't tell the difference between me and your ex, then I don't know what we're doing here."

They stood in silence for a long time. Sara couldn't look up, couldn't look at this face. It was as if she was paralysed. She could hardly tell what was real any more.

A large ginger cat jumped down from his perch on the dining chair and walked across the room.

"I should go," Nate said.

Before Sara could think what to say to him, he was gone.

CHAPTER TWENTY-FIVE

Sara regretted the argument as soon as the door closed behind him. He hadn't meant to upset her. She certainly knew how easy it was to let things slip out in the heat of an argument. If he'd been defending her to Moana, as he'd said, well, it was still a betrayal of trust but an accidental one and done for noble reasons.

As for letting him think she believed him capable of violence towards her...that was her own baggage, not his. The look of hurt in his eyes when he'd seen her flinch was almost more than she could bear. She couldn't punish him for Greg's mistakes. Or her own.

"Nate, wait." She hurried after him and made it through the dining room door when one of the cats ran between her legs, tripping her. "Damn it!" She reached out to catch herself and a bolt of electricity burst from the ring on her hand, crackling down the hall to shatter the pane of glass in the front door. Shards of glass rained down over the polished wood floor like crystal hail.

The cat purred.

"What the hell?" She stared at the ring, trying to see any sign of magic or power in the gemstone's depths. She remembered the vision she'd had of Bridget and the Maori women in the basement, summoning up the stone vines with their chanting and the power of the fae ring. She remembered what Jereth had said about it in Bridget's memories: that it could access his power.

"Shit!" Sara tugged at the ring, trying to pull it off her finger. It stuck on her knuckle, sharp edges digging into the skin. "Shit shit shit! Get off!"

The cat growled.

A wave of dizziness washed over Sara as Bridget's ghost appeared again. "Stop," the whispery voice of the dead woman said. "The ring protects."

Sara shook her head against the ghost's words. "This is so messed up. You're dead! This is ridiculous. I can't be part of this. It's too much."

The metal circle slipped past Sara's knuckle and off her finger. Her skin tingled and sparks fountained out from the wall sockets.

"At last!" A voice rang in her mind. A voice deep and earthy as tree roots. "It is time for us, Sara. Come to me now."

CHAPTER TWENTY-SIX

Nate tried to put Sara O'Neill out of his mind as he lifted a large, cardboard delivery box onto his electrical supplies counter at the store. He'd stuffed up royally. There was no doubting that. The question was, could he fix it?

The store was empty but for Abigail, drawing on some scrap paper in the corner and Moana at the main counter. The rows of groceries between them seemed colder than the frozen section. She would come around though. For all her faults, Moana was a woman who believed in family.

Sara, on the other hand, he was less sure of.

She was wounded from her last relationship. He'd known that. Hell, if he were to give advice to anyone else in this situation, it would be to stay clear. So why couldn't he take his own advice? There was something about her that drew him in. Something that made him feel things he hadn't felt about any other woman since Emma.

She was different to the women he knew in town.

Interesting, talented, and so incredibly strong and capable in ways she wouldn't even acknowledge to herself. He felt happier in her presence than he had felt in a long time. Working together to save her house made it feel like they were partners. He'd been surprised at how much she knew and how capable she really was. Somehow, even wielding a sledgehammer and covered in dust, she exuded femininity and strength in a mix that was as distracting as it was sexy.

It'd been a shock to find her on the floor this morning. Whether she'd collapsed or merely fallen asleep there, he wasn't sure, but seeing her like that had made his heart feel as though it were being electrocuted. When she'd woken up and been nothing but angry he wasn't sure whether to laugh or cry.

His intentions of making amends for anything she'd heard of his and Moana's fight, however, were quickly dashed and when she'd actually flinched away from him…the memory of it made his chest ache still.

He stabbed a pen into the packing tape on the box and ran it along the crease, breaking the seal. He pulled back the flaps but barely saw the collection of batteries, fuses and other items inside.

He'd only meant to offer a hug. To soothe her somehow and apologise for his mistake. Instead he'd made it worse.

"Daddy." Abigail tugged on his sleeve. "When am I going back to Sara's house? It's boring here."

Nate sighed. "I don't know, honey. Soon, I hope." Better to give her some space today.

"I drew her a picture." The little girl held up a drawing of a house surrounded by cats.

He chuckled. "I'm sure she'll love it."

The chime on the door sounded, announcing the presence of a customer. Nate caught himself looking up eagerly, hoping it would be Sara. Instead a dark haired man in his mid-thirties, wearing jeans and a buttoned up dress shirt paused to look over the store, then made his way to Moana at the main counter. He had a photograph of a car in his hand.

Nate sighed and turned back to his delivery. He pulled out a carton of double A batteries and a couple of watch batteries he'd ordered in especially for Sara, given how much trouble she was having with her watch.

"Excuse me," he overhead the man saying. "I don't suppose you've seen this car anywhere in town have you? It was stolen about a month ago and got snapped by a speed camera not far from here."

"Sorry," said Moana. "I'm not really into cars."

"Fair enough." The man's voice was warm and charming. "What about this woman?"

Nate's head snapped up. Why would a stranger in town be asking about cars or a woman? There was only one new woman in town within the last month.

"Oh yes, I know her," Moana was saying, her finger tapping the second photograph. "That's Sara O'Neill. Right piece of work. She's who took your car, is she?"

"I'm afraid so."

Nate waved frantically, trying to catch Moana's attention. She glanced at him and he shook his head. "No," he mouthed silently.

Moana smiled sweetly. "Head North. First road on your left, then third right. Hers is the last house on the road."

The man picked up the photographs. “Thank you. You’ve been most helpful.”

“Want me to call the police?” Moana asked.

“No, that won’t be necessary. I’ll just get what’s mine.” He slid a fifty dollar bill across the counter. “For your trouble.”

“Moana, you idiot!” As soon as the man was gone, Nate threw his stock items back in the box and shoved it under the counter. “What did you do that for?”

“Do what?” She raised her chin defiantly. “Tell a man where his stolen car is?”

“Did you think for a second about what I told you yesterday about Sara’s past? The car isn’t stolen. It’s just registered with her ex’s name and address. That’s the man who put Sara in the hospital and killed their unborn baby!”

Moana’s face went grey. “Oh God. Are you serious?”

Nate’s lip curled. “If you weren’t so caught up in your petty rivalry you’d have realized how suspicious that was. You’ve just handed her over to a madman. Now close the shop. We’re going to go fix this.”

CHAPTER TWENTY-SEVEN

Sara stared into the water of the circle pool. Ripples on the surface traced patterns that sparkled with light. Will-o'-the-wisps danced in the periphery of her vision like reflections from a mirror-ball. The twisted tree in the centre swayed and she could feel the being trapped inside it reaching out to her.

"Welcome," it said. "You came at last."

Sara blinked and looked around. "How did I get here?" She didn't remember the walk. Didn't remember the bush or the path. Only the deep earthy voice, calling her on. "Jereth?"

The tree shivered and leaves fell from its branches, making tiny green boats on the surface of the water. As they fell, the leaves traced patterns of light in the air, a filigree of glowing threads. When they were done, she could see they were woven into a pattern – the form of a man with a beautiful face, golden hair, and shining green eyes.

"I've been here for so long, Sara," he said. "Set me free."

Her head felt light and dizzy. He was so beautiful. She couldn't get enough air in her lungs. Couldn't breathe. "How?" she gasped, slowly dropping to her knees before him, tearing her gaze away from his face and staring into the water at his feet.

"Give me back my ring," he said. "The traitor witch has used it against me long enough."

"I'm no traitor." Bridget's ghost drifted out of the trees. The fae seemed not to see or hear her, but her presence helped clear Sara's head. "Don't give him the ring, child. It is all that protects this world from his kind."

Bridget had never spoken so much before. Sara shook her head. It was as if she was drunk somehow. It was so hard to think clearly. "Why? How are you talking to me?"

Bridget smiled. "You forged a connection between us when you entered my memories, Sara. I'm more real in the world now. For a little while, at least."

"The bindings on me are weakening," said Jereth, obviously thinking her question was meant for him. "But they are not yet gone. Help me and I will reward you when my people are free."

"But…" Sara fingered the hard edges of the ring in her pocket, struggling to think. "I don't think I should."

"Do it," Jereth urged her, and at the sound of his voice her body leaned forward closer to the water. "Throw the ring into the pool. It is mine. Let me have it back."

Sara waivered. "You hurt people. You killed Bridget's nana." She thought of her own grandmother, back at the retirement home in Auckland. How could she free a man who would hurt an innocent old woman? How could she free any man who would hurt any woman? She climbed to her feet and backed away from the circle. "You hurt Bridget. You're just like Greg. So, no! You can rot in hell!"

Jereth roared in frustration. A blast of wind shook the surrounding trees and the will-o'-the-wisps stopped in their tracks and shivered. "Wait! And look." He pointed at the pool.

A ripple traced over the surface of the water and when it cleared, Abigail lay at the bottom of the pool. Her eyes were closed, her face peaceful. Her chest rose and fell with regular breaths as she slept under the water.

"Give me the ring and I will give you back this child," Jereth said.

"Don't listen," Bridget whispered. "Don't trust him."

Jereth's face twisted with annoyance. "You think I don't see you, witch?" A crackle of lightning leapt from the water to strike the ghost. She dissipated like mist. "If not for your lover's child, Sara, what of your own?"

Sara looked again and Abigail held a baby in her arms. The tiny child held her arms up toward Sara, miniature fingers clasping at nothing, reaching for her mother.

Sara gasped. It was a blow to her chest. Everything she'd felt in the hospital flooded back. The despair, the loss, the pain. The judgement. Her child had left this world rather than be with her in the home she'd made with Greg. Her whole body felt constricted with the guilt.

"You could save her, Sara. You could make her

safe." Jereth's voice was soft and seductive.

"Stay strong, Sara," Bridget whispered in her mind. "It's not real."

But what if it was real? Could she really take that chance? Her child was dead and yet…so was Bridget. That didn't stop the woman participating in the world. What if Jereth could bring her daughter back?

"Can you do it?" she asked. "Can you really bring her back from the dead?"

"Give me the ring, Sara," he whispered. "Set me free."

She stared at it. A small circle of gold and gemstone in the palm of her hand. Such a small trinket to part with. Such a small price to pay.

She held it out over the water.

From somewhere behind her, a voice began to sing. The words were unfamiliar, but the sound rang true somewhere in the depths of her mind. *Te reo. Maori.*

Sara turned and saw Moana striding towards her from the bush, her eyes wide circles of white, but her voice strong. As she sang, the will-o'-the-wisps faded, the water grew still, and Jereth's image against the tree grew faint.

Sara felt her mind clear of the fae's influence. Abi and the baby in the water were gone – they had only ever been illusions. Never real. Her eyes blurred with tears. She closed her hand over the ring and drew it back.

"Put it on," Bridget's voice whispered in her mind. "It will protect you both."

Sara slipped the ring onto her finger once more and it was as if someone had switched off a radio. The static in her mind was gone. Jereth's thrall was broken.

She stumbled back from the water's edge and

Moana caught her.

"You're all right now," the Maori woman said. "He almost had you."

"But..." Sara stared at the other woman. "What are you doing here? I thought you hated me."

"I thought you were here to call that creature forth," Moana said. "But I just saw you fighting him. I thought you needed help."

"Thank you." Sara swallowed. Her hands were trembling. "We need to get out of here."

"We can't." Moana pointed back toward the circle. Jereth's image was growing stronger again, clearer. The tree behind him beginning to appear translucent. "He's getting free. We have to stop him."

"But...how?" Sara searched the clearing frantically. There was one person who knew what was going on. One person who had been here from the start and knew Jereth better than anyone. Who had trapped him over a hundred years ago. "Bridget! Come back. What's happening? Tell me what to do!"

The ghost appeared instantly, almost solid in appearance, but for her eyes. When Sara looked into Bridget's eyes, she could see the green punga branches behind them.

Moana gasped and took a step back, then nodded. "Help from an ancestor. A good plan...for a *Pakeha*."

"Without the ring, Jereth will seek energy to free himself," Bridget said. For once her voice strong, as it had been in life. "The fae manipulate energy. That's why they have always been associated with illusion and madness – energy in the form of light or bioelectric energy in the brain. But with the industrial age came electricity. Energy everywhere – in every house. Every building. All linked together. At first they couldn't manage it – the effects of iron and other metals conducting that energy made it difficult for them to handle. But they learned, Sara. They learned! That's what's been draining your batteries. That's what killed the man from the power company. The portals in the old world have been closed. The fae have been reaching out through this portal, this new country, looking for electricity – and you gave it to them by wiring up the house!"

"But…I didn't know. Why would you leave the house here if it wasn't safe to hook up to the grid? Nobody has a house without electricity any more."

"Because we need the house. It is part of the spell that binds the portal closed and Jereth trapped in it. Jereth helped us build that house. The *kuia* and I used it as a solid doorstop, preventing travel from the other realm. The ring he gave me powered the spell and the local iwi have always added their strength as well. But you took the ring and the protections have been steadily failing ever since!"

Moana stared. "Wait, you mean the house is part of the protections? Why didn't I know this?"

Bridget shook her head. "Your sister became sloppy with her duties. She should always have had a fully trained family member ready to take over if she perished. But she was young. She never believed she would die before she had a chance to teach her daughter about the entrance to what you call *Rarohenga*, right in her own back yard. If she had told you, Moana, you might have prevented this instead of trying to destroy my house."

The Maori woman swallowed. "I only knew some of the details. I knew the O'Neill family brought the *ira atua* with them and created the portal to their world. I thought the house was part of the portal. I didn't know it was part of the block."

Sara touched her shoulder. "There's no sense worrying about that. What's done is done. What can we do about it now?" She held up her hand. "What if I put the ring back where I found it? Would the house start protecting us again?"

The tree in the circle writhed and shrieked like a howling wind.

Bridget nodded. "Yes. But you must do it quickly. There's not much time." She turned to Moana. "You are your family's *kuia* now."

"Me?"

"You're all that's left. You must stay here and continue the chant. Perhaps it will delay Jereth's escape."

Moana took a deep breath and nodded. "I'm sorry I misjudged you," she said to Sara, her jaw tight. "Let's do this." Without waiting for a reply, she strode back towards the circle and began to sing.

"Good luck," Sara called after her.

"You must go," Bridget said. "Take the ring back to the basement as fast as you can and do not take it off until you get there. It will protect you from Jereth's illusions. But not for long."

Sara ran as fast as she could towards the house. The branches and ferns whipped at her legs and face but she ignored them. Will-o'-the-wisps flew across her path, shot at her head and fountained sparks at her from all angles. Her eyes were dazzled and vision spotted with strange coloured lights, but she kept on. The power in the ring made her immune to the fae's attempts to turn her around.

"Get away," she shouted, and felt a pulse of energy wash out from her body, pushing the lights and visions back into the trees. The ring on her finger glowed softly for a moment, then winked out.

"I'm getting better at that," she muttered.

The trees parted and the house was up ahead. She'd left the generator going and a light was on inside, spilling the warm glow out onto the porch and deepening the darkness outside.

Electricity. Energy the fae could use.

Not if she could stop it. She headed toward the generator. She could turn it off now and be safer inside the house.

A figure stepped out of the shadows and swung something at her. Her back exploded with pain. She stumbled, and fell, her knees scuffing painfully on the ground. The figure swung again. This time she saw the plank of wood from the discarded pile of construction debris at the back of the house in time to raise an arm to protect herself. The wood connected with her elbow with a sickening crack. Sara screamed.

The figure laughed. She knew that laugh.

"No!" Horror filled her to the brim, icy and paralyzing, pressing on the inside of her skin with chilled fingers. "No!"

Greg stepped forward into the light. "Hi, Honey. Did you miss me?"

CHAPTER TWENTY-EIGHT

The low hum of the generator was a soft backdrop to cicada song as Nate got out of the car. The sun was already starting to set, throwing long shadows across the house and turning the bush from friendly nature park into sinister wilderness. A strange car was parked behind Sara's in the drive. Greg was already here. So was Moana. She'd driven off at great speed while he'd been buckling Abigail into her seatbelt. There was no sign of either of them now.

"Stay in the car," Nate told Abi. "Lock the doors and don't open up for anyone."

Abigail's eyes were wide. "I want to come with you."

Nate shook his head. There was no telling what he was going to find if the man searching for Sara really was her ex. "You're safer here, kiddo. If you get scared, beep the horn, okay?"

The front door of the O'Neill house was open and there was a light on in the lounge. A ginger cat stared at him from on top of a hall table, daring him to come inside.

"Sara?" he called. "Is everything okay?"

The house was silent.

She'd been so angry with him this morning when he'd come inside to check on her. Doing so again so soon felt like an invasion of privacy but the gnawing in his stomach that said she was in danger wouldn't let him stay still. He hurried inside, moving quickly from room to room, calling her name.

"Damn it," he muttered to himself, pulling out his phone to shine the flashlight app into the dimly lit corners. His stomach felt like he'd swallowed batteries and his shoulders were tight as coiled wire. "Come on, come on. Where are they?"

Somehow, in the few short weeks he'd come to know her, Sara had become a mainstay in his life. Every day was brighter because she would be there to talk to at the end of it, whether it was just to pick up Abi after work, or to stay for a couple of hours working on the house together. This house, that had been empty for as long as he could remember, now represented fun and laughter and, if he dared admit it to himself, love. It was a feeling he never thought he'd experience again after losing Emma. Now he feared he might be too late to keep from losing it again. The house was empty once more.

Empty, and the door open.

"Shit!" If Sara had been surprised by Greg, she might have made a run for it. They might not be inside the house at all.

The overgrown yard was dark with shadow. The phone flashlight did very little to illuminate more than a couple of feet at a time. He circled the house once, and found no sign of anyone. He crept closer to the edge of the trees, eyes straining in the increasing gloom. He called Sara's name a couple of times but was answered with silence.

True silence. The cicadas were quiet. There was no twittering of birds or rustling of creatures in the leaves. A chill passed through him, raising goosebumps on his skin.

Then a sound pierced the night and electrocuted him with terror.

The long, panicked toot of a car horn.

CHAPTER TWENTY-NINE

Sara scrambled across the grass, heedless of the dirt sticking to her clothes and fingers. Her elbow was agony but she pulled herself along, ignoring the worried part of her mind that screamed it could be fractured.

"It's not possible," she said. Her voice was fragile and splintered. "How could you find me?"

A flash of lightning lit the sky and she saw Greg's smile as he advanced on her. "I'll always find you, babe. You know that."

She did know it. Somehow she'd always known it. No matter how much she had wanted to convince herself she was safe here, there had always been the fear, the knowledge, that it had been too easy to get away. All the kind words and support from the nurses, counsellor, and her grandmother meant nothing in the end. She'd tried so hard to get away from that life and start anew and yet here he was, pulling her back in. Why did she think she could escape?

The world seemed to narrow around her, hazy,

heavy, and hot. Her chest was tight and her head felt fuzzy, the way it did when Jereth's mind control had taken her into the bush and almost forced her to unlock the portal. The ache in her lower back reminded her of the pain she'd been in the last time she'd seen Greg.

When she'd lost their child.

The thought was an electric shock running up her spine. It galvanised her. She would not let Greg or the Fae control what she chose to do with her life. She would not let her child's death be in vain. Her response surged up from her abandoned womb, from her gut and her soul. "No! Leave me alone!"

She surged to her feet and ran. She had escaped him before, she would do it again. Her breath was raw in her lungs as she heaved one foot in front of the other, her aching elbow clutched close.

Greg's footsteps were close behind and Sara's mind raced ahead, seeking the safest path. Even as she headed for the house, she knew its safety was an illusion. She reached the porch and vaulted the stairs. The door was ajar but even if she could get inside and close it, there was no way the old lock would withstand much force. She passed it by without even slowing, hoping that the move would confuse her pursuer, even if only for a moment.

She reached the end of the porch and jumped, gripping the railing hard as she did so. She sailed over it and onto the lawn beyond, and, as it had done with Moana a few weeks earlier, a chunk of rotted railing broke away in her hands.

Greg, caught off guard and not expecting to jump the railing, was trapped on the porch and would have to back track to the stairs.

Sara threw the broken piece of wood in his general direction and ran toward her car.

She never saw if it connected but heard him swear and a clattering sound as it hit the floorboards of the porch.

The few moments the manoeuvre had bought her were wasted when she realised her car was blocked in. Moana's car, Greg's car, and Nate's ute were all in a row like deadly beads on a string, keeping her trapped.

"Shit." She ran for the last one in the line, Nate's ute, and grabbed at the door handle, hoping against hope he had left the keys in the ignition. The door was locked.

A small, brown face appeared at the window.

Sara yelped and jumped back. "Abi?" She glanced behind her. Greg was gaining ground. Behind him, a flash of light, like a torch, bobbed in the distance, near the generator. Probably a will-o'-the-wisp. She couldn't trust it. Nothing was safe. Except maybe Abi if she stayed in the car. She turned back to the girl. "Stay there," she said and ran for the road.

The gravel crunched underfoot like teeth chewing through bones. Larger, heavier teeth crunched ever closer as Greg gained distance behind her. The hesitation at the cars had eaten into her lead.

A car horn blasted through the air like an air raid siren. Abi was signalling for help. There was no way it would come in time.

Nate's house rose out of the darkness ahead and Sara swerved toward it, hoping that her knowledge of the grounds would work to her advantage.

The lights in the house flickered like visual static, the bulbs barely holding a charge before fading out only to brighten up again, like dying glow worms clinging to life. The air crackled with the energy flowing out from the portal pool. The fae were reaching out into the world. She could feel it. Their energy scraped across the landscape, seeking purchase. The wires in Nates house were responding to their call.

She ran around the side of the house, ducking through the garden gate and into the courtyard at the back. There was the verandah where she and Nate had eaten dinner together. The wash of warm memory flooded over her with the scent of freesias and daphne.

Her footsteps faltered. Could Nate be home? Could he help her escape? No. His car and daughter were at her house. And there was no point bringing danger to him now. Greg was her problem. Running was the only solution.

"Gotcha!" A rough hand gripped her shoulder and shoved.

Sara lost her balance and stumbled. Her shoulder grazed along the side of the house and she fell.

Greg loomed over her. "No more running," he said.

Sara felt the wall against her back, hard and unforgiving. She was cornered. She swallowed. Her chest was tight and her pulse pounded in her ears. She pushed back, somehow hoping the planks would part and let her through. "Don't," she said, her voice soft. "Just…don't."

The flickering lights showed the smirk on Greg's face as he opened his mouth to reply. Before he got the words out, his eyes bulged and he screamed. "What the fuck?" He swatted at his back with his hand, spinning away from Sara, deeper into the courtyard.

On his back was the tiny, black and white form of Oscar, the kitten, clinging tightly.

A deep yowl came from the direction of the fence and a big ginger tomcat launched itself at Greg. A grey blur of fur brushed past Sara and began raking Greg's legs with its claws.

More and more of the cats that'd been loitering around her home swarmed Greg, with claws and teeth and hisses. It was as if he'd kicked open some feline hive and the cats were defending their queen.

Sara stared, open mouthed for a moment, then got to her feet and ran back to the road, leaving Greg and the cats behind.

She rounded the corner and Bridget was there. But this time it wasn't just Bridget.

Sara squinted her eyes. There was another figure within the shape of the ghost. "Abi? Oh my God. What have you done?"

The ghost and girl both nodded. Sara could now see Abigail's body clearly inside the translucent Bridget. "She is safe," Bridget-Abi said. "I could not reach you this far from the house without a vessel."

"A vessel? You've possessed her?"

Bridget shrugged. "In a manner of speaking. She is her mother's daughter after all. She has the gift."

Something clicked into place in Sara's mind. "The woman she said used to live at my house. She could see you."

Bridget nodded and the double-image waved a hand impatiently. "You must return to the house. You must reactivate the spell."

"But Greg..."

"Is nothing compared to the horror that is waiting to break through into this world. Be brave, my child. You must hurry."

Sara fiddled with the gemstoned ring on her finger. The fae engagement ring. Bridget had sacrificed so much to protect the world from Jereth and the creatures beyond the portal. How could she give up now? "Okay."

Lightning flickered across the sky, casting the combined figure of Bridget and Abi into sharp edged colour. In that moment, the magic that bound them schismed. The little girl screamed and clapped her hands over her mouth. Bridget's eyes widened. "Behind you!"

Then something hard hit the back of Sara's head and everything was black.

CHAPTER THIRTY

The shadows in the bush thrown by what light was left in the darkened sky had nothing on the terror that punched into Nate's gut at the sound of the car horn. It jolted him like a live wire. Even before it ended, he turned and ran for the driveway. There was only one reason Abigail would sound the horn like that: Danger.

The distance from the edge of the trees, around the side of the house, to the car felt like a marathon. The silence after the horn was deafening. Finally, Nate rounded the corner and the car came into sight. The passenger door was open. His daughter was gone.

"Abi! Abi!" Nate turned in circles, his gaze raking the darkness. His chest felt like he was being electrocuted. It was hard to breath. "Abi? Sara? Shit!" He fumbled his cell-phone out of his pocket. With Sara's ex here and now Abi missing as well, there was no telling what had happened. He punched the numbers for the police. The phone crackled and disconnected.

He dialled again.

Lightning flashed across the sky.

The phone screen flickered and went black.

"No, no, no." What was it about this place that drained the batteries of things? He rummaged in the car for a charger. Nothing. "Damn it."

He thumped the steering wheel and barely felt the pain. How could they have just vanished? Abi, Sara, and even Moana. His body felt hollow, the way it had when he'd heard the news that Emma had been in an accident. It was the feeling of loss and helplessness. They were gone. Gone and there was nothing he could do.

He gritted his teeth. "Not this time." He wasn't ready to give up yet. The landline at his house would be working. He'd call the police from there and have the whole area swarming with searchers in minutes.

He turned the key in the ignition and the sound of the engine turning over almost drowned out her voice.

"Dad. Help!"

He shot out of the car and stared into the darkness. "Abi?"

The sound was coming from back toward the bush behind the house. A light bobbed among the trees like a torch. "Dad!"

Then Sara called as well. "Nate! Over here."

His feet barely touched the ground as he hurried after them. "Are you okay? What's going on?" He followed the light into the trees, always just a little too far behind to make out who was carrying it. "Wait up," he called, but they kept moving forward, deeper and deeper into the bush, mysteriously silent.

Then, horrifyingly, the light blinked out. Spots appeared in front of his eyes as they adjusted to the darkness.

The spots resolved into lights in a clearing ahead. A few steps later, Nate stepped out of the trees into something impossible.

The clearing contained a pool of water that glowed like the moon and bubbled as if boiling. In the centre of the pool, a stunted kauri tree twisted and groaned, its branches reach out towards the women who surrounded it. They were old, Maori women, in a range of clothing styles from traditional woven flax fibre to seventies garb. They were singing in their own language, a melodic chant of some kind and stood, unflinching, as the tree thrashed against them, clearly fighting their song.

"What the…?" Nate stumbled forward, feeling a sudden pity for the tree. "What are you doing?"

Lightning burst upward from the pool, spiking into the night sky. The shock of illumination showed clearly what he had not seen before – the women were transparent! All but one.

The one solid woman turned to face him. It was Moana. His sister in law had tears rolling down her face as she sang. "You shouldn't be here," she said, breaking off from the song. "Sara is the key. She's back at the house. Go to her."

He frowned. "But I saw…" He hadn't seen her. He'd only heard. It had been a trick. "What's going on?"

"Go!" Moana said through gritted teeth. "Run!"

Around her the ghosts all threw back their heads and screamed.

Nate ran.

CHAPTER THIRTY-ONE

Sara forced open bleary eyes, her brain fighting against the pounding in her head for consciousness. She remembered very little after Greg had hit her again. A familiar tickle on her cheek told her she was bleeding. Her arm ached almost as much as her head, but those seemed to be her only injuries. She'd had worse.

Her body was on a hard surface, cool and smooth. Floorboards, her mind told her. He'd carried her inside.

She blinked a few times and her vision cleared. She was in one of the upstairs bedrooms. The door creaked open and Greg appeared, a small form in his arms. He bent and laid it on the bed.

Abigail lay still where he left her, her eyes wide and fear filled. She was gagged and bound at her hands and feet.

Sara's heart sank. She hadn't realized Abi was here. God knew if Greg would draw the line at hurting a child.

"Just close your eyes, Abi," she said softly. "Think of this as a game. It will be okay."

Greg turned at the sound of her voice. "You're awake. Good. You can explain what the hell you think you've been doing. Do you have any idea what it was like to have some policeman knock on our door and hand me a piece of paper that says I'm not allowed to speak to you? Or to have to chase my wife down some country road? Hmm? You think you've got the right to take my money and my car and spread stories about me like that? After everything I've done for you?"

Sara wiped the blood from her face with her sleeve and pushed herself up into a sitting position. "It wasn't your money, Greg. It was my share. And I didn't spread stories. I just told the people I needed to tell so that I could move on. I can't be with you anymore."

"Why?" His fingers curled into fists.

Sara felt her chin tremble. She knew what those fists could do. "You know why."

He stared at her for a long time, jaw jutting, breathing hard through his nose. "You know we argue," he said at last. "We always have. But I don't mean to get angry with you. You just do the stupidest things, Sara. Like this running away bullshit. I mean, what the fuck am I supposed to do when you pull something like that?"

"Let me go," she said quietly. "Let me live without being scared all the time. If you loved me you'd give me that."

He snorted. "Yeah, well, if you loved me you wouldn't be such a bitch all the time."

"I'm not…" Sara let her voice fade. This was the pattern, she realized. This was what would give him his reason to hit her again. If she argued, he would feel justified in getting angry. If she stayed silent, he would assume she would do as he said and be angry if she varied from it. Two paths to the same outcome. She couldn't afford to travel either of them. "The girl isn't part of our issues, Greg. She's just the neighbour's kid. You can let her go."

He paced, back and forth, between her and the door. "I don't think so. She was tooting the horn in the car outside. I think she's gonna be a little bitch about it. We need to sort out our issues first."

"Okay." Sara stood up, her muscles ached and her head was spinning, but she forced herself to smile at him. "Okay. We can sort it out. Just…I think she's scared, you know? She's just a kid." She reached out and touched his arm.

Greg froze, staring at her hand.

"What the fuck is on your finger?" His face was red and eyes bulging. "That's an engagement ring. Sara, who the fuck gave you an engagement ring?" His fist clipped her jaw and sent her flying backward. Her knee caught on the edge of the bed and she fell, landing across Abigail. The little girl screamed into her gag.

Greg advanced on them both. "You're cheating on me? That's what this is about?"

"No, Greg, no!" Sara sat up, pushing at him, trying to keep herself between the advancing man and Abigail's wriggling body. "It's not what you think."

Greg snatched at her hand, pulling the ring from her finger. He held it up to the light. "What is it then? Hmm? It looks like you ran away with another man, Sara. So who is he?"

Outside, a peal of thunder rolled across the sky and

lightning lit up the window. Sara felt the dread in her stomach intensify. She had no idea how long she'd lain unconscious or how long Moana's chant would slow down the fae. Jereth was breaking free.

"Greg, please, give it back." She couldn't keep the urgency out her voice and reached for the ring but he jerked it back out of reach.

"Why? Do you love him so much already?" He sneered.

She shook her head and reached for it again. "It's not from another man, I promise. But I need it back." She left her hand out, palm up, waiting. "Please?"

The window lit up again, this time the thunder came after the lightning. Green lightning, like spring leaves sheeting across the sky.

Greg's lip curled. "I don't think so." He casually backhanded her across the face.

Sara twisted as she fell, moving with the force of the blow with instinct born of experience. Resisting would only make the damage worse. Nevertheless, her cheek ached with the shock of the blow and the cut on her brow started bleeding again.

She braced herself for the next blow but it never came.

"Hey," a familiar voice bellowed.

Sara's breath caught in her chest.

Nate stood in the doorway, his muscular body framed by the wooden beams like an avenging forest god of builders. His biceps stretched the fabric of his t-shirt. His right hand held a hammer. His eyes were dark as he took in the scene before him and settled his gaze on Greg.

"Leave them alone."

CHAPTER THIRTY-TWO

Sara watched as Greg circled around, keeping his eyes on Nate like a shark, waiting his chance to strike. "So, no other man, huh, Sara? Lying bitch."

"I didn't say there wasn't another man," Sara said quietly. "I said the ring wasn't from him and I didn't cheat on you. Those are both true. I met Nate after moving here."

"Whatever." He turned his back on her. "So you're the big hero are you?"

Nate kept his arms spread. "Just looking out for a friend. I think you should leave now."

"Is that so? I think you should mind your own business."

Sara saw the tension in Nate's face. The muscles in his jaw went hard. "You've kidnapped my daughter and you're hurting someone I care about. This is very much my business. Get out."

Greg's gaze flicked from Nate, to Sara, to the hammer. "Fine. You want the dumb cow, you can have her." He walked toward the door.

"The ring," Sara called out. "I need the ring back."

Nate turned to look at her. "What ring?"

Greg took advantage of his momentary distraction and swung his fist at Nate's head. His fist connected with a crack and Nate stumbled back. The hammer dropped from his fingers and clanked on the floor.

The second blow was aimed at his ribs. Nate twisted his body to one side and returned a blow of his own. Then another.

"Like to beat up on women, do you?" Nate growled. "How is it with someone who hits back?"

Greg grunted as the air left his lungs. He lowered his shoulder and charged back at Nate. The two men collided, crashed into the wall, and fell, pummelling at each other with their fists.

"Stop it. Stop!" Sara grabbed Greg's shoulder and tried to pull him back, but he jabbed back with his elbow and caught her in the stomach. The jolt of pain made her gasp. "Damn it, Greg!" She slapped at the back of his head over and over again. "Get out! Get out, get out, get out!"

The lights flickered and sparks fountained from the wall sockets. Outside, thunder boomed, drowning out the sounds of struggle.

The men rolled and Sara found her legs swept out from under her. The three of them tangled like eels in a creek before breaking apart, panting for breath.

A glint of light shone from the floor at the foot of the bed. The fae ring.

Sara reached for it, but a vice-like hand gripped around her ankle and pulled her back.

"No you don't," Greg growled.

"Leave her alone!" Nate grabbed the other man's wrist, trying to force him to let go.

Sara turned, twisting her leg in an attempt to get loose. She saw Greg's hand raise up behind Nate, holding the hammer. "Look out!" she screamed.

Nate jerked back, but not quickly enough. The edge of the hammer grazed his skull, just above the left ear, and he slumped to the floor.

"No!" Sara scrambled to Nate's side, putting herself between him and Greg. "Nate? Nate? Are you okay?"

He moaned.

"It's okay, Nate." She pulled him into her arms, cradling his head. "You'll be okay."

Greg spat blood onto the floor and sneered. "Oh, isn't that sweet. You're such a whore, Sara."

Lightning crackled outside and the house shook with the impact. Whatever was happening at the circle was intensifying. If she didn't reactivate the spell in the basement soon, there would be no stopping Jereth and his hordes from breaking free.

She lifted her chin and met Greg's eyes. "Then why are you bothering with me? You've had your revenge. Just give me back the ring and leave us alone."

"Perhaps I will." He scooped up the engagement ring and stared at it for a long time. The hammer dangled loosely in his other hand.

Sara held her breath.

Greg set the ring down on the dresser. "Do you love him?" he asked.

Her fingers clenched on Nate's shoulder, feeling the hard muscle beneath his torn t-shirt. Her heart trembled as the answer spilled from her lips.

"Yes. I think I do."

Greg raised the hammer.

"Tough."

He brought it down hard on the ring.

CHAPTER THIRTY-THREE

The gem shattered. A blinding flash of light and energy burst through the room. Greg screamed as green electricity surged up his arm from the hammer and threw him back across the room. His body hit the wall, twitched several times, and lay still.

Through the window, Sara could see the sky was alight with ripples of colour. The generator exploded, shooting a geyser of flame up into the air, yet the lights stayed on. Sparks showered out of the wall sockets in rainbow colours, singeing carpet, bedding, and clothes alike wherever they landed.

Throughout the house and yard, dozens of stray and neighbourhood cats began to yowl, a haunting chorus of feline voices, revelling in magic's awakening. Beneath it all was a low rumble, like a rockslide of gemstones: Jereth's laugh.

Sara stared at the flattened and broken remnants of the fae ring – the one last thing between Jereth and his freedom. Terror sawed at her insides with sharp, serrated teeth. Greg was nothing to what Jereth could do. She scraped at the squashed gold.

"Oh God, oh God." She could feel her breathing race and her stomach cramp. "Bridget! Bridget! What do I do? The ring is gone. What do I do now?"

The ghost appeared, sparks rippling down her skirt like silver embroidery. She took in the destroyed ring, the unconscious men, the terrified Abigail, still bound on the bed. She closed her eyes. "It is too late," she said, her voice low and whispery once more. "He is coming."

The wind howled louder and louder and the glass in the window burst inward, shattering in a rain of crystal pieces all over the room.

Sara screamed and covered her face. When she looked again, Jereth stood where the window had been.

He was every bit as beautiful as she remembered from Bridget's memories, but his face was cold and hard. The light that played around him like tendrils of glowing mist seemed filled with glittering fragments of ice.

"You could have been on my side, Sara," he said. "I would have rewarded you. But you are the same as all your human kind. Vapid and scared. You don't deserve this land."

Sara looked at Bridget. The ghost woman seemed smaller somehow. Bent, even. As if Jereth's presence had broken her. She wouldn't look at him, staring instead at the golden flakes and shattered gemstone that were all that was left of the ring she had worn as a sign of her love for the fae.

At her feet, Nate stirred. He reached up and touched her hand. Sara closed her fingers around his, feeling the warmth of him against her skin.

She realized she was no longer afraid. The worst had come to pass, but she had weathered the worst before. She had suffered beatings and abuse. She had lost her child and felt the bite of rejection. She had endured guilt, pain and heartbreak. And she had survived and found love again. She had Nate. He might be injured and there was a good chance they wouldn't survive this, but she knew he cared for her. He had come to her rescue when no one else could. He had faced her demons with her and that demon, Greg, lay unconscious on the floor. Magical or not, she knew what the fae were. She had struggled with their kind for years of her life. Not anymore!

"You're a bully." She spoke the words clearly, strongly, with no shaking in her voice. "You're stronger than us, and you're a bully. Why did you even pretend to be in love with her if you were only ever planning an invasion?"

The fae frowned. "Why did I pretend? Oh, human, that's rich. Ask your precious witch who it was that betrayed our love first. It was not I who was the trickster here, but I've had nearly two hundred years to pay for my folly and consider my revenge on your kind. Two hundred years trapped in a tree while my treacherous lover ran free with my power bound up in the symbol of my love!"

Bridget looked up at that, her eyes blazing. "You murdered my grandmother! Who does that to someone they love?"

"Lies! Human deceit and lies!" Electricity crackled around the edges of the room, turning the house into a kind of faraday cage. On the bed, Abigail whimpered and curled into a ball.

Nate let go of Sara's hand, crawled over to his daughter and pulled her into his arms.

"You see that?" Sara said. "Family is important to us. You're angry that Bridget trapped you when you're threatening to kill everyone we love?"

"That was never my intention," Jereth snarled. "But why shouldn't I after what was done to me? She lies so sweetly, this one. My Bridget. She was the bait for my trap. The nectar for my honeybee. And this bee will sting when it is cornered."

"She's not lying," Sara said. "I've seen her memories."

The fae lord's head tilted and he stared at her. "Have you indeed? Then see mine." He threw out his hand and a bolt of lightning shot from it, straight to Sara's heart.

"Don't hurt her!" screamed Bridget, and leapt at Sara. The world dissolved in a spray of colour and they tumbled into memory together.

Sara watched as Jereth strode into the clearing and up to the circle, his long, loping stride easily covering the distance of two or three of Bridget's Nan. The old woman wore a sturdy brown woollen dress under a feathered shawl given to her by the local Maori.

"You seem to be gaining respect with the natives of this land," Jereth commented. "It must be good to have your skills appreciated once more."

"It is," said Nan. "But I learn as much from them as they do from me. Our ways are both of the earth but...different."

Jereth nodded. "Differences can enhance each other

when brought together. I've discovered this myself during my time with your family."

Nan shot him a sideways look. "I've noticed."

"Ah." He nodded. "Bridget has spoken to you of our feelings."

"She has."

"It is one of the things I will speak with my people about today." He gestured to the circular pool of water encircled by four saplings and several large, flat stones. "You have my thanks for building this portal. It will mean a great deal to us."

She nodded. "Step into the water, my lord Jereth. I will open the gap between realms."

As soon as his ankles sank into the cool water, Jereth knew she had lied. The feel of the portal was wrong. There was no gentle opening that he could step through. The water pulled at him, tugging him deeper like a whirlpool.

He turned. Bridget's Nan was crouched at the edge of the circle, her hand digging into the earth like claws. Behind her, Bridget's father stepped out of the trees, an iron poker in his hands.

Jereth tried to step out of the water but his legs were trapped. Magic was holding him, pulling him to the centre of the circle. "Stop this. What are you doing?"

Around the circle, brown skinned women with straw skirts and tattooed faces were emerging, their voices raised in chant.

"We had a deal," Jereth said.

Nan lifted her head, her eyes black with magic. "And it did not include my granddaughter! Did you truly think we would allow you to wed? Be gone back to your own realm, creature. You will never see Bridget again!"

Sara felt the pain in Jereth's chest. The agony of loss mixed with the physical tearing of his very being from the human world.

"No! Bridget! I love you! Bridget!" He flung all that he could into a psychic message but the combined force of the women present was too much. The magic doubled back on itself, echoing in his mind.

The door between worlds was closing. He flung himself forward, lashing out with all the power at his disposal. Lightning exploded throughout the clearing, wild, uncontrolled. The circle closed and he was trapped, ever reaching. Ever alone.

CHAPTER THIRTY-FOUR

"Sara? Sara? What's happening?" Nate's voice was the first thing she heard as the world resolved back into the present. The memory of Jereth's terror and loneliness left tremors in her body.

"He was so alone," Sara whispered. "She never pushed him back through to his people. He was fighting too hard to get back to Bridget. That's what trapped him between worlds with no one. All that time with no one and she kept him there."

"Nearly two hundred years," Jereth said. "You kept me in that hell because your family refused to let us marry?"

Bridget sobbed, the ghosts tears tracing translucent streaks in her skin. "I didn't know," she said. "They told me you had betrayed us. Your lightning killed my Nan."

"No." Jereth shook his head. "She died from over reaching her magic. I refused to give up fighting to come back to you and she refused to stop holding me back. The exertion was too much for her, but she wore me out enough that I couldn't speak to you when you came. And then it was too late. You believed their lies so easily."

Sara felt a tug on her sleeve as Nate pulled her to his chest. He rocked her there, letting the warmth of his body sooth the chills of the borrowed memory. She clung to him as the ghost and the fae argued above them.

Slowly, something else came into her awareness.

"Nate," she whispered. "What's that smell?"

He kissed her temple before answering in a soft voice, directly into her ear. "Smoke. The house is on fire. We need to get out of here."

She gasped and shifted in his arms, but he held her tight.

"We can't move yet. Look."

She turned and saw what he did. If anything, Jereth's power had increased while she had experienced his memory. His pain and anger were being channelled into waves of electricity, pulsing around the edges of the room. Webs of lightning covered the door and the window, making escape impossible without certain death. Thick black smoke was seeping in, pooling across the ceiling like molasses sticking to the lid of the jar.

"What about Abi?"

"She's here." The little girl huddled next to her father, her eyes wide. "But we need to get out of here or that smoke will suffocate us. Who are these people?"

Sara pressed her lips to his, hard, brief, passionate. She put everything she had into that kiss and let it beg him to trust her. "Get ready to move."

She stood up.

Bridget and Jereth continued to argue, the lines of electricity pulsed in time with his words.

"Jereth, you need to let us go," Sara said. "Now."

He looked at her, his eyes red. "Why?"

She gestured around them at the burning house. "Because we're trapped here. Just like you were trapped. But we'll die!"

He turned away. "So?"

Bridget met Sara's eyes for a moment, then nodded. She laid a hand on Jereth's arm. "I know that's not the real you, Jereth," she said. "You respect life. It's one of the things I fell in love with."

He said nothing.

"Please, Jereth." Sara took a deep breath. "I felt your pain in that memory. I know what it was like for you. But Nate and Abigail had nothing to do with what happened. They're not O'Neills. And I love them. Please let them go."

"Look at the child, Jereth," said Bridget.

He snorted. "A human child. Why should I care about that after what your kind did to me?"

She shook her head. "Not that one. Look closer. At this one." She pointed at Sara.

The fae frowned, peering at something in Sara's face. "No. It cannot be."

"It is," Bridget said.

Jereth's eyes widened. "Bridget, my love. You bore me a child!"

"What?" Sara blinked.

Bridget smiled at her. "You're not my great niece, Sara. You're my great great grandchild."

CHAPTER THIRTY-FIVE

Sara gaped. "How is that possible?" Everything she knew about Bridget said the woman had died a spinster and never had children of her own. But if she and Jereth had consummated their relationship…could the family have kept something so significant a secret?

"I should like to know that as well." The electrical display around Jereth dimmed, the web of lightning around the room darkened, but did not vanish. Behind it, a new threat loomed. Flames licked at the edge of the doorframe and the window was a sheet of fire, the outside wall of the house already fully alight.

Nate scooped his daughter up and draped her over his shoulder. "Sara, we can't wait here. We have to go. Now!"

Jereth held up a hand. "Wait. I will hold back the fire while we hear the answer. Fire is only energy after all and we fae are the masters of energy."

Nate and Sara exchanged a glance. "I want to know," Sara said.

He nodded.

Bridget reached out and touched Jereth's hand. "I was already with child when you were taken from me," she said. "I had no knowledge of what my family planned to do. I truly believed they would let us be married. When I saw that my Nan had died…" She closed her eyes. "I'm sorry for what I did to you. I didn't know you were innocent."

Jereth swallowed. His eyes were shining. "And the child?"

"My family wanted to dispose of him, but I wouldn't let them. In the end, they agreed to raise him as my brother's child. He married young and the deception was complete. I stayed a spinster and watched over our line until they moved away." She gestured to Sara. "Until this one returned."

Tears slid down Jereth's face. "I have descendants? You know how difficult it is for fae to have children?"

Bridget nodded. "I do, my love. The connection must be one of perfect love and even then, carrying the child is difficult. Our children suffered the same, but they survived."

Sara felt the tears in her own eyes, though they felt hot with the heat of the flames. She was part fae and the fae had trouble carrying children to term. Her daughter had not abandoned her. She had not left because of guilt or judgement. There was a reason. She was not alone.

She felt Nate's hand squeeze hers.

The roar of flames and cracking of burning timber grew louder. She took a deep breath and gagged on the smoke in the room. She coughed, her lungs burning like acid.

"Okay, we really need to go," Nate said. "Whatever you people are, I need to get Sara and Abigail out of here now."

Jereth touched her shoulder. "Come my child. Let me see you and your family to safety. Bridget has been your guardian long enough. It's time for me to do my part."

The lightning cage vanished.

"Thank you," Sara said. "Great grandfather."

Nate urged her toward the door. The frame was black and cracked, fire gripped it in tiny, dark orange fingers. Beyond, the hallway walls were well ablaze. Heat washed over Sara as if from an oven. Fear rose in her as she looked down that hall of flame. They'd waited too long to escape. Even as she watched, the banister on the stairs crumbled. Any moment the stairs themselves would follow. There was no way to get through the fire to freedom now.

Then, as she watched, the flames receded, dying down to barely embers. The heat rolled back like a carpet, pulling much of the smoke away with it.

"Hurry," said Jereth, his voice tense. "I will keep it at bay as long as I can, but the fire is wild already."

Sara glanced back. The fae's eyes were narrowed in concentration.

Bridget took his hand. "I will help, my love," she said.

"Come on," Nate said. He led the way down the hallway, careful to step between the little patches of flame that were already burning in the floor boards. Sara followed in his footsteps.

Somewhere below, she could hear a crashing sound

as some beam gave way and part of the house collapsed. A burst of sparks flooded up the stairwell, pushed by the force of the collapse. She hesitated.

"Come on," Nate urged her. "You can do it."

"We have you," said Jereth.

Together, they hurried down the stairs and the flames in the hallway below died down before them. Each door they passed held a room burning like a furnace, but their path was clear, made safe by Jereth's power as he followed them through the house.

At last, Sara could see the front door. Their portal to safety and freedom. She breathed a sigh of relief.

A moment later, a wall of flame burst forth, blocking their path. The fire ran along the ceiling at lightning speed, the hallway quickly starting to burn.

"No!"

Sara spun to see what had happened.

Jereth's back was arched, his body stiff and his face contorted in a silent scream. He twisted, and dissolved, his body splitting into tiny flecks of light that scattered in the wind.

Greg stood behind him, brandishing the hammer. He swung it again and Bridget's ghost vanished as well, disrupted, as Jereth had been, by the iron in the metal hammer.

"You're not free to go until I say so," Greg snarled. "And I say, you can burn, bitch."

Nate bent over to put Abigail down but, Sara waved him off.

"You know what?" she said. "I can deal with this idiot."

"You sure?" he said. The flames were growing on

the walls again and the heat was rising. There was no clear way out.

Sara smiled. "Yeah. 'Cause it turns out I'm the descendant of a crazy Irish witch and a pissed off fairy prince. And you know what that means?"

She reached for the power she'd seen and felt Jereth manipulate in his memory. Feeling her way as he had, she pulled it up out of the earth beneath them, out of the sky around them, out of the electrical wiring in the walls, out of the flames that were destroying her home, and out of the portal pool in the bush, now a wide open gateway to the other realm. She held out a hand and it was filled with a crackling ball of power.

"It means my abusive ex is shit out of luck!"

She thrust the power at Greg and it exploded into his chest. His eyes went wide as he was blasted backward, crashing into the burning staircase. A cascade of soot and embers rained down on him.

Sara turned and held out her hand. The flames between her and the front door died. "Let's get out of here," she said.

CHAPTER THIRTY-SIX

Moana joined them outside as they watched the house burn. She stood a little way away, leaning on her car, arms folded. Her clothes were muddy and torn but the orange glow of the flames painted the angles of her face and made her appear noble and arcane. She nodded to Sara, a simple gesture of approval and support.

Sara nodded back. She had managed to get them out safely with her newfound powers over energy, but she had been unable to save her home. Nate had used her phone to call the fire department but there was little chance they would arrive in time. He stood now with his arms around Sara, holding her close. Abigail clung to them both.

Sara could feel the warmth of his body sink into her through their torn and sooty clothes. The scent of him was comforting and right.

She couldn't believe they had argued only that morning. It seemed a lifetime away.

She turned and snuggled her face into his neck. "Thank you," she said. "For coming to save me."

His arms gripped her tight. "Thank you," he said. "For saving Abi and me."

She chuckled. "Any time."

He pulled back a little and, for a moment, she was afraid of what she might see in his face. There was nothing but concern. "That thing you can do," he said. "Does it hurt you?"

She shook her head, smiling. "No. Not at all. But I'm not sure how much I'll be able to do after the portal closes."

"Is it going to close?" Nate asked. "What about Jereth's invasion?"

Sara closed her eyes and reached out for her great great grandparents. She could feel them on the other side of the circle, in the other realm. They felt happy. They'd found each other again. They were content. She could feel that other world slowly withdrawing from this one.

"I don't think it's going to be a problem," she said.

A large chunk of the porch roof collapsed, sending embers flying into the air.

"I'm sorry about your house," said Nate.

Sara shrugged. "I'll rebuild. I was starting a new life anyway."

"I'd like to be part of it," he said.

A smile crept across her face. "You sure? There's probably going to be a lot of cats. They're attracted to magic you know. And apparently I *am* magic."

He grinned back and leaned in to kiss her. His lips were firm and warm, and left a tingling sensation where they had touched. She melted against him, sinking into the embrace.

"I always thought you were," he said.

THE END

AUTHOR'S NOTE

Thank you for taking the time to read my book. I hope you enjoyed reading it as much as I enjoyed creating it.

Please consider posting a review or telling your friends about this book. Word of mouth makes a huge difference to an author and is greatly appreciated.

If you'd like to read some of my other work or keep up to date with future books, you can check out my website, join my e-mail list, or follow me on Facebook or Twitter. You can also check out my short story collection, *Shifting Worlds.*

Website: www.darian-smith.com

Facebook: DarianSmithAuthor

Twitter: @DarianWordSmith

ABOUT THE AUTHOR

Darian Smith lives in Auckland, New Zealand with his wife (who also writes) and their Siamese cat (who doesn't).

By day, he works with people who have neuromuscular conditions such as muscular dystrophy or charcot marie tooth disease. He is also a qualified counsellor/family therapist and can be seen – by those very swift with the pause button – on television shows such as Legend of the Seeker and Spartacus.

For more information about Darian and his upcoming work, please check out his website at www.darian-smith.com.

SHIFTING WORLDS

A collection of short stories by Darian Smith
Foreword by Jennifer Fallon

Drag queens fight zombies.
An immigrant artist hopes love conquers all.
Deep space explorers wrestle with an alien artifact.
A superhero is locked in an insane asylum.
These 16 stories span the worlds of fantasy, sci-fi, and literary fiction, and cause the characters' worlds to fundamentally change. Includes several prize winning stories as well as some that are seen for the first time in this collection.

"Never fails to entertain and surprise…this collection has it all" – Jennifer Fallon

Excerpt:

There's a moment, just before waking, when I forget it's gone. I feel the ghost of it on my shoulders, the warmth inside. It boosts my confidence and makes me stronger. I am more myself. I am ready to rule the islands and mould the day to my bidding.

Opening my eyes is a disappointment. My old bones ache with craving. It's been missing from me for almost three decades, but I feel it just the same. I'm simply an old man with his memories and regrets. I had my chance. I was not worthy.

Get your copy at Amazon.com & selected bookstores.

www.ingramcontent.com/pod-product-compliance
Ingram Content Group UK Ltd.
Pitfield, Milton Keynes, MK11 3LW, UK
UKHW041955190726
13854UKWH00005B/1977